"McGowan's debut novel has a stronghold on surrealist storytelling and a mastery of language as an artform. If you've ever pondered your finite and fluid relationship with time, this book is for you. Timeless Gardens & Other Beautiful Miseries will tug at the heartstrings you didn't even know you had."

Glen Binger

author of *Head Games: The Novel and Figment.*

"Timeless Gardens is spellbinding and so beautifully imagined that I wouldn't have put it down for anything. McGowan is able to compellingly balance heart-cracking grief and the triumph of the human spirit. He writes this fantastical tale with lucidity and honey-smooth lyricism. The characters are written with such tenderness that you are tempted to reach into the pages, pull them out of the book, and wrap them in woolen blankets. In his novel, McGowan reminds us what it means to be fully alive, even in the face of tragedy, hardship, and loss. It left me eviscerated and marveling, and for that it is a book I will return to."

Jacqueline Bird

author of *Taste Life Twice.*

"Between his birds-eye view of our connection to the universe and his fly-on-the-wall insight into human nature, McGowan is a master of perspective who makes you question if you've ever truly seen a person at all."

Lauren Eden

author of *Laying You to Rest, Atlantis, The Lioness Awakens,* and *Of Yesteryear.*

"Superb! T.J's writing is captivatingly time-bending and intriguing. Enchanting and wildly suspenseful, Timeless Gardens & Other Beautiful Miseries, will grab you immediately and propel you into a world of real-life misery mixed with magic. It will take you on a fanciful journey through time—one that is both delightful and fascinating. This beautifully written tale of pain, peace, and transformation will alter your reality and leave your mind wandering in a timeless world of wonder and sorrow. Highly recommend!"

Natalie Nascenzi

author of *Out of Chaos, The Aftermath of Unrest,* and *Isle of Skye.*

TIMELESS GARDENS

& other beautiful miseries

TIMELESS GARDENS

& other beautiful miseries

T.J. McGOWAN

iiPUBLISHING

Acknowledgements

I am nothing without the love and support of my mother and sister. They are immovable forces in the cheer section of my life. The Crawdad Crew for always letting me disrupt the group chat with some abstract ideas about the world of poetry and storytelling and how insufferable I find all of humanity(except for them). Leah, a human that makes humaning seem worth it(unless it gets too peopley out there), with constant words of support for both my creative and regular life. To the British truck that planted the seeds of this idea in my head one random night. Tonii for giving this odd little time twister a home, and providing me with an amazing, caring, and dedicated editor in Saba. Lady Birdsmith for reading draft after draft over the years, constantly pushing me with the most thoughtful feedback. Jade always telling me I rock when I did not feel like I rocked, especially when the writing started to drag. My dude, Glen, and his incredibly insightful comments, which further enhanced the final manuscript. Lauren, whose open ears and kind words made me tap into a sense of pride for my talents when the goal seemed far out of reach. Merceades for listening to my doubts and turning them around. My therapist for, well, the obvious. And lastly, but not leastly, Jen. This book does not exist without you. Nearly two years and almost twenty drafts later, here we are. Your input, advice, editing skills, clarity, encouragement, and compassion for these characters, is etched into the very core of this book. It would still be collecting dust if not for you and our need to stay sane in a fucking pandemic. All of these people, and many more, make me feel brave in a cruel world.

Foreword

There's magic held in the everyday. Sparks of existence that startle you. Sedate you. Make you feel like the fibres have separated for you to step into, even just for a moment.

That's what T.J. does with this story. He challenges you to bring life into the very now. To confront every fear with a question, to embrace every emotion with humility. His words invite you into what it means to become alive. You read him, to become yourself.

When T.J. initially spoke to me about the book he had been writing, it was during a time when it felt like the magic had gone in our everyday life. We each suddenly had our own walls to contend with, to live amongst, to try and fill with art, music, stories, meaning. Fortunately for me, I was lucky enough to be given the first draft of Timeless Gardens, and, with it, I felt that flicker.

From then on, lots of notes and scribbles and conversations ensued between the two of us about who these characters were. What their lives meant. What the words could give out, particularly during a time when everything felt so heightened and uncertain. What I loved was that T.J. always readily welcomed any feedback. I quickly became aware of just how much T.J. cared about these people. His passion and knowledge of scriptwriting helped give these characters a voice. His raw talent as a poet built their layers and connections. The kind-hearted, complicated, compassionate, and pure human in him made these words into a story.

This tale spiders out and threads itself back in. It brings wisdom and tension, calmness, clarity, and revelations. It tumbles you and then centres you.

I've had the honour of not only watching this story grow but seeing T.J. grow. He's found the magic. He is the magic.

And he's letting you in.

~ **Jennifer Johnson**

Hollow Hills

There are seeds of nature we sometimes plant to beautify the ugliness of the world; a dressing up of what we wish to avoid or deny. And there are seeds of nature that simply occur, without deliberation or remorse or a desire to be understood. They are and always were. As people, we become entangled in their mysteries and secrets, acutely aware of our imprisonment to what we will never know about the hands of the universe we sleep in; only rationalizing time by the gaps between our tragedies and triumphs, only able to grasp experience in limited endeavors that lead us to laugh and cry, in repetition, until the only guarantee we have sweeps us, our questions, and beliefs, into oblivion. Mortality is always teasing from the shadows while we search for ways to turn grief to growth, and paint pictures from the colorful wells of our collective sadness. Welcome to Hollow Hills, where some become more entangled than others and, for Ellis Foster, time often seems like it forgets to exist...

The Long Way Home

❦

Winter 1950

A loud bell signals day's end at Hollow Hills Elementary School. Less than a hundred students spill from small classrooms in the single-floor building; some walk alone, others come together in groups, their voices resounding in the school corridor. They're all bundled up in winter gear, from coats to hats, to mittens and earmuffs. Some wear leather-bound backpacks. Others alternate between carrying their books loose or strapped together with a belt. The brigade of delighted children makes its way out onto the sidewalk where parents await to bring them home.

The sky is gray and spotted with somber clouds. The trees along the streets are bare and the ground is covered in a thin layer of dirty snow. Ellis Foster, ten, pushes through the crowd and walks home alone, his dark brown hair falling over his soft eyes. He doesn't have a backpack and tucks his schoolbooks under his arm. The boy's beige slacks are wrinkled and dirty along the bottoms. The corduroy coat he wears is tattered from time and the hat on his head seems much too big for him. A gust of wind rides along the street and slaps him in the face. He wraps his scarf tight around his cheeks.

Ellis crosses the street into the busiest part of town. He stops at Esterman's Deli, a small corner grocer, and pays a couple of quarters for a handful of candy and a can of apple juice. He enjoys the treats as he passes several businesses and town landmarks.

St. Sebastian's, a small Catholic Church, stands across the street with its doors closed. The Roundabout Diner, crowded with teenagers sucking down root beer floats and milkshakes, caddies the corner at the end of the street. The following block houses a desolate playground and various other shops that line the center of Hollow Hills.

At the end of main street, Ellis heads south toward the waterfront, which can be seen clearly from the top of the steep hill he stands on. Docks sit between a few, narrow warehouses and the ocean. Most of the boats, moving in their place along the waves, are covered for winter, except for a couple anchored and being unloaded by workers. To the left of the docks is rocky terrain below a tall, imposing cliff. And, beyond the water, in the faint distance, rests another town on the horizon. A power plant protrudes through the gray on its shoreline. Halfway between it and the docks of Hollow Hills is a small approaching ferry. Pickup trucks and delivery vehicles haul wares back north, away from the docks. A few workers walk uphill on the opposite side of the street, all passing one cigarette back and forth to puff on.

Ellis casually enters the docklands, throwing his candy wrappers in a trash can outside a small office at the entrance. The rough and tumble man seated at the window of the office nods in familiarity to Ellis. "Landing three," the man says. Ellis smiles and nods in accordance.

The boy surveys ahead with squinted eyes. Through the commotion of workers, he spots a tall, gruff man with a wiry red beard and bushy hair barely kept under control by a wool cap. The man is loading a wooden pallet with bags of chicken feed. He notices Ellis but continues slinging the bags. A veil of disappointment waltzes across the boy's face.

"Why aren't you home?" the man asks, never stopping his work.

"I forgot my key this morning, pa."

His father looks up, frustrated. His eyes are deep brown, almost black. Gateways to more trouble than triumph. The edge of a faded scar on his leathery forehead pokes out from under his hat.

"Foster," a dock foreman yells in their direction.

The father looks at the foreman and straightens up to talk to him.

"Can't have kids running around here. You know better than that, Mike," the foreman grumbles.

Michael Foster acknowledges his boss and looks back at Ellis. "Go and wait for me in the truck," he barks, as he tosses Ellis the keys.

Ellis watches the sunset from the driver's seat of his father's beat-up truck. Bored, he puts his hands on the steering wheel and pretends to drive. He cuts the wheel hard in either direction, making acceleration and brake noises with his mouth. Laughter shakes his tiny body as it bounces up and down on the seat. At the height of his fun, Ellis is startled quiet by the sneering reflection of his father's face in the dashboard mirror.

The boy promptly shuffles to the passenger's seat. His father gets in. Ellis avoids eye contact. Michael twists the key in the ignition to start the truck and drives off without a word. The vehicle clunks up the hill and bears left into town, traveling past all the closed stores. Down a quiet street it pulls over across from Johnny's, a cantankerous looking pub with a group of dregs chain-smoking and spitting tobacco out front.

Go with God

Winter 2031

*L*aura Nagan, loosely clutching a rose, stands before a tiny coffin hovering over a hole in the earth. Her black dress ends below her knees, making the small-framed brunette seem taller than she is. Lines that echo from the laughter of better days are beginning to find permanence on her face. The focused grief in her eyes keeps her at a spiritual distance from those gathered around her.

Frank Nagan stands next to her. He is nearly twice her height, clean-shaven, with kind, hazel eyes struggling to maintain control. He wears a black suit, seldom taking a glance at his mourning wife. Their shoulders ever-so-slightly turned away from each other in a position that suggests frigidity has long been a part of them.

"Go with God now, young William," the priest says.

Frank and Laura break at the words, as do others in the small crowd.

One after the other, the group visits the burial site to place their rose atop the coffin. Frank and Laura approach. People stand in a silent group behind them. Frank remains a foot or so away from the coffin. Then, he places his hand on it. Overcome with emotion, he covers his face with his other hand to catch his tears before stepping away.

Laura leans in and kisses the coffin. Her eyes are dry and bloodshot. Her stare barely shows signs of life. She whispers goodbye. With her head still on the coffin, she catches a glimpse of a portrait of her son on a nearby stand. He is smiling, with bright blue eyes and neatly combed brown hair. Across his bust it reads: *William Henry Nagan (June 15, 2024 - November 22, 2031)*

Laura's face curdles at the sight. She darts her head in the other direction and cries. When she lifts her head to leave, she can't help but notice a younger man, a few rows away from her, staring. He wears a green-knitted sweater over all black clothing, with dirty blue shoes. His hair is short and his face clean-shaven. He's not the type to stand out in a crowd, but his voyeurism can't go unnoticed. Their eyes lock. A few seconds pass until the moment stretches into discomfort and he looks away. Her eyes retreat. Her painful reality kicks back in. She takes one last look at the grave and then heads toward the cars.

Extra Ketchup

— 🍎 —

Winter 1950

*J*ohnny's has a scattershot of locals sprinkled about under low lights, tending to their drinks, and carrying on conversations many of them will soon forget. In walks Michael with Ellis at his heels. As they approach the bar, the father trades a few greeting glances with others.

On the other side of the counter is Marilyn, a redhead in her forties, wearing a loose flannel shirt, the sheen in her eyes out of place in the company she keeps. She pops open a beer and slides it towards Michael. He nods with gratitude and takes a sip.

"The usual, handsome?" Marilyn playfully asks Ellis. He climbs up onto a stool, shaking his head yes, reciprocating her smile.

Marilyn yells into the kitchen behind her, "Burger and fries, extra ketchup." Then, she turns back with a Coca-Cola, removes the bottle cap and hands it to him with a wink. Ellis blushes.

"Foster, how goes it?" She directs her question to Michael,

placing her hands on the rim of the counter.

Michael picks up his beer and takes a sip. "Another day, another dollar, Mare," he says, exhausted. His eyes scan the room and halt on a dark-haired woman seated at the end of the bar, who already has her sight set on him. About the same age as Michael, she is alone, smoking a cigarette over a martini. He tosses a subtle acknowledgement her way and takes another sip of his drink.

"There she goes! Your biggest fan," Marilyn teases, following Michael's gaze to the woman.

Ellis watches the woman and his father exchange glances. She's dressed fancier than the others in the bar. A white blouse sits tight to her body. Flashy jewelry wraps around her wrists and neck. The makeup on her face is apparent and peacocked around her eyes. She gets off her stool and moves closer to Ellis, taking a seat by his side. "Ellis, my favorite gentleman," the woman says. She flicks her cigarette into an ashtray on the bar.

The chef brings out a plate with Ellis's food and places it in front of him. A burger and fries with extra ketchup, just like he wanted. He digs right in.

"Can I get you another, Blanche?" Marilyn asks.

Blanche steals a fry from Ellis's plate, slathers it in ketchup, and bites it. "The question is, can he get me another?" she counters flirtatiously, staring at Michael.

Marilyn shifts her gaze towards Michael, fighting the urge to laugh. Michael concedes and she proceeds to mix Blanche's martini. Blanche takes a big sip to finish her current drink, then gets up from the bar and saunters toward the back, placing a few quarters in the jukebox. Swing music fills the dank little bar. Blanche sways and dances alone; a couple of the men in the bar ogle her from their seats. Michael turns his back to the bar and watches along, sipping from his beer. Blanche rotates her hips, ignoring all the other men, locked onto Michael.

"The hunter being hunted," Marilyn jokes. Michael pays her no mind, his eyes fixated on Blanche. Ellis can't control himself and laughs, the ketchup dressed on his teeth.

Michael places his beer down with force, startling Ellis. "Nothing funny, son."

The stern look on his face quietens Ellis. Then, he slides Ellis's plate toward himself and picks up his burger, ravenously biting into it. Marilyn's discomfort is impossible to hide.

"You want to laugh at your old man? You can figure out how to feed yourself."

Michael finishes the hamburger and slides the plate back in front of Ellis. All that remain are a few French fries. Ellis folds into himself with embarrassment.

"Give the kid a break, Mike," Marilyn interjects.

Michael finishes his beer and asks for another. He walks off with it and Blanche's martini to a table occupied by two other men. Blanche shimmies over in the direction of the table.

Marilyn lowers her head over the counter to match Ellis's eyeline. "You know, your father wasn't always like this," she says in a comforting tone. Ellis raises his head, relaxing the tension in his body. "He used to be really nice. Almost unbearably so. But his heart hurts. And sometimes when a person's heart hurts, they take that pain out on the other people they love," Marilyn says.

"Why?"

"Well, handsome, because it's easier than getting better," Marilyn admits.

Ellis stretches his neck around to see his father flirting with Blanche, who is now sitting on Michael's lap. Marilyn taps the bar top to get Ellis's attention. "Here's a thought. We get you home with another order of fries for the road. What do you say, handsome?"

Ellis lights up at the thought.

Missing Things

❡

Winter 2031

*F*rank Nagan sits in his pickup truck, idling in the driveway of his two-story home. The radio is off, and he sulks in the silence with a toy plane in his hand; its color indiscernible in the darkness. Gently, he uses a finger to knock the front propeller to make it spin. He watches until it stops and puts the plane into his glove compartment and closes it.

He turns off the truck and uses a remote to open the garage, revealing a sleek, dark SUV with a silver sun emblem on the hatchback handle. He gets out with a bag of groceries and places them on the hood of his truck, then reaches in to remove his work bag off the passenger's seat. The moon is up and glowing across a clear sky. Its fullness is reflected in the massive solar plate stretched across the roof of the house. Impossible not to notice, Frank looks up. The stars spread out like pin pricks in a black tapestry as far as the eyes can see.

The wind kicks up and chills him.

He enters the house through the garage and places the groceries down on a tool bench when he notices the SUV isn't plugged into its charger. He fiddles with a touch screen on a charging station against the wall in front of the car to reset it. He pulls a retractable, single-prong cord from below the touch screen. At the hood of the vehicle, he pops a twist lock and inserts the prong into an outlet. He checks the screen once more to make sure the charge is taking.

The door creaks as he enters the house. Frank commands the downstairs lights on with his voice. The interior of the house is a mix of modern and bohemian. An array of distinct color schemes fills in the walls. The newest gadgets and electronics sit fixed between bold art and plant life. It straddles the fence of a time between a future fast unfolding and a past worth holding on to.

He places the groceries on the dining room table and heads down a nearby hall into a guest bedroom. He puts his bag down at the foot of the bed. The room is sterile looking with some basic furniture and nothing much on the walls. Piles of his clothes are scattered about on the floor, which he quickly tidies up onto a recliner opposite the bed. He takes a quick shower in the bathroom connected to the bedroom and changes into a sweatshirt and pants.

In the kitchen, he unloads the bag of groceries on a pristine and sizable island in the center of the massive space. The refrigerator boasts double doors with a touch screen display and small TV on its front. To its right, on another counter, a high-end cutlery block filled with stainless steel knives caddies a massive spice rack. State-of-the-art digital cookware is neatly positioned all around. Every type of cooking tool, pot, pan, and plate occupy the counters and cupboards. Frank removes a large pot from a cabinet below the island and a medium size pan from a rack hanging over it. He places them both down on the stove top. Then, he proceeds to bring all of his sauce ingredients over and starts adding them to the pot. He begins mixing but stops abruptly and places the spoon down on the counter.

Frank, now at the top of the steps of the second floor, can see the door at the end of the hallway is open. The light inside is off. He makes his way down into the other room.

Laura is under a children's blanket on a bed shaped like a spaceship. Frank turns on the light. The walls are completely decked out in posters of planes, spaceships, and other various flying machines. Different model planes are parked on the windowsill. The room is immaculate.

"Did you eat today?" Frank asks.

Laura doesn't answer him.

"I'm making Penne. I'll leave some out for you, for later."

Frank heads back downstairs and meticulously puts together the meal, savoring every step of the process. Everything is accurately measured and timed and executed to perfection. He sits and eats alone on a stool at the island. A show he doesn't pay attention to plays on the display screen of the refrigerator.

He cleans up after himself and goes to put the leftovers away, but there's no room in the fridge when he opens it. More than a dozen different types of Tupperware occupy the shelves, each filled with some kind of casserole or comfort food. One-by-one he pulls them out and places them on the island to put his pasta away. He turns back toward the island and is startled to find Laura at the entrance between the dining room and kitchen.

"What are you doing with all this?"

"Tossing it. It's been almost a month. Most of it has mold and I need to get the Tupperware back to their rightful owners." Frank says.

Laura walks to the refrigerator and removes Frank's pasta. She fixes herself a plate and puts it in the microwave while Frank scrapes old food into the garbage. The two of them say nothing to one another as the microwave hums along for two painful minutes and finally beeps. Laura takes a seat at one of the stools and eats. Frank moves the empty Tupperware containers from the island to the sink.

"You need to remember to plug the Icarus in when you get back home," he tells her.

"I barely use it."

"More the reason, because then it sits with no charge."

Frank turns the faucet on and begins rinsing the containers.

"Have you seen his plane?" Laura asks.

"Huh?" Frank replies, as if he didn't hear her.

"His plane. It hasn't turned up."

Frank shuts off the water and turns, facing Laura's back. "I'm sure it will," he says.

Laura finishes another bite. "I've looked everywhere. You don't remember where you last saw it?"

Frank takes a deep breath. "In the box. The one the cops gave us after they were done."

Laura fights back tears.

Frank continues, "You know, we really need to talk about the suit as well. That poor woman. I don't know if we can keep putting her through this."

Laura drops her fork into her plate and takes a deep breath before leaving the kitchen to go back upstairs. Frank grabs her plate and brings it to the sink. He turns the water back on and continues cleaning up. Afterwards, he heads straight for bed in the guest room. Alone, in the darkness, he stares at the ceiling. In one, swift wave the agony contorts his face, and he cries himself to sleep.

In Billy's room, Laura sits on the edge of the bed, dressed in a winter coat and snow boots, smelling his blanket. A meek smile breaks on her face as she takes in the aroma. Moments later she places it back down on and leaves the room.

Downstairs now, in the dining room, Laura watches the arms of the clock on the wall methodically tick into the future. Whisky melts ice in a glass sitting beside a pen and pad in front of her. She opens the pad to a blank page and stares into the white abyss. She grabs the pen and nervously swings it between two fingers, knocking it against the page.

In Order to Survive

Winter 1950

*E*llis wakes in bed to the sound of a thud from below his room. Muffled voices push their way through the floorboards. He pulls back his blanket, sits up in his bed, and turns on a lamp. *Stuart Little* lay open on his lap from before he fell asleep. He dog ears the page and places it on the nightstand next to a framed photo of his father, who appears much younger and happier, standing next to his mother, a pretty brunette with a gentle smile.

His room is sparse. A twin bed with musty, white sheets sits between two simple wooden end tables. A mismatched, black dresser hugs the wall opposite his bed. It has a small radio atop it, with a few stacks of books on either side. A mirror in the corner has a few postcards sticking from its frame. The walls are covered in brown and white wallpaper and a few hand-drawn pictures Ellis created.

He gets out of bed and carefully walks to the door as the

noises get louder. His tiny hand gently turns the knob. He slowly exits into the empty upstairs hallway and peers down the steps at the end of the hall, into the kitchen. A sharp light splashes across the floor below. He sneaks to the bottom of the staircase and follows the shaft of light to a knocked-over lamp in the living room. Shadows dance on the wall; figures moving together to moaning voices.

Ellis adjusts his eyes to the sounds. His father has Blanche on a counter that sits between the living room and kitchen. Michael's arms grip her bare back, while his head is buried in her neck. She giggles between her panting. His head raises from her neck and, through the darkness, he spots Ellis.

Ellis quickly runs upstairs and amidst his fright, stubs his toe against the door. Without giving heed to the pain, he runs to his bed in a panic. He curls into a ball, covering himself in his blanket, his eyes forced shut. The noise outside the room picks up again. The woman's giggles get louder as the two adults stumble through the hallway, into another room. A door slams shut.

***

The next morning, Ellis gets up with the sunshine climbing its way through a window to the right of him. He rolls out of bed, rubs his eyes vigorously, and heads downstairs to make breakfast: bacon, eggs, and toast. He puts on a pot of coffee. Then, he sets the table for three and waits at his seat.

By the time anyone arrives at the table, things have gotten cold. His father descends the stairs alone, dressed in a white t-shirt and underwear. He walks to the kitchen sink and fills a glass with water. Digging around a nearby drawer, he pulls out a bottle of aspirin, pops two into his mouth, and notices Ellis at the table mid-swallow. Michael doesn't utter a word and sits across from Ellis. He sees the third place setting.

"That kind of woman doesn't stay for breakfast."

He breaks the yolk of his eggs with a piece of bacon and

crunches it between his teeth; some of the yellow slime coating his lips and getting into his beard. Ellis cuts into his egg with the side of his fork and takes a meager bite. The two of them eat in silence. When Ellis finishes, he gets up and brings his plate, along with the extra food, to the sink. His father grabs his arm.

"Going to waste it?"

Ellis looks at the full plate of food, then to his father.

"Sit. Finish it," his father commands.

Ellis obeys and returns to his seat.

"When you're done, get dressed and meet me out back."

After washing the dishes, Ellis goes to his room to clean up his bed. He grabs *Stuart Little* from the nightstand and sits at the edge of his bed with it. He peeks through his window into the backyard. Michael is holding up a small hide full of fur. The fence behind him is lined with drying animal pelts. Ellis opens the book defiantly, but another look at his father outside causes him to quickly close it and place it back on the shelf. He puts on a pair of dirty pants and a shirt covered in paint stains.

Outside, his father directs him to stack a load of chopped wood in a pile near the backdoor. Once all the wood has been neatly stacked, his father waves him over to the shed, where he removes two rifles still in their leather cases. He hands one to Ellis, who hesitantly takes it by the straps.

"Time you start earning your keep around here," his father asserts. Michael opens the case to his rifle, a Winchester Model 70. Ellis places his case down next to his father's and opens it. Inside is a brand-new Savage 99.

"Don't be afraid of it. It's yours," Michael says. He removes the Winchester to stare down the scope. Ellis removes his rifle from the case, studying it for a couple of seconds. Unsure of what to do with it, he puts it back. Michael lowers his firearm.

"Pick it up. We hunt this weekend," he says.

"But I don't want to...," Ellis says.

"You don't want to what?" Michael insists, not letting him off the hook.

"Hunt," Ellis admits, bracing for his father's reaction.

Michael swings his rifle onto his shoulder and kneels before Ellis. The boy notices the hardening on his father's face, his scraggly beard and eyes holding memories of better days. "You don't have a choice. We all do things we don't want to in order to survive. That's life. It's not your fantasy stories. It's hard and unapologetic. Cruel and mean. It has no interest in what you want. Now pick it up, get to know it, and focus on the task at hand."

Dr. Tree

Winter 2031

*L*aura walks through town, past quiet houses and lonely streets, until she reaches the Hollow Hills playground. Her breath floats in front of her as she sits in a swing, eyes closed, listening to the wind sweep around her. She gently sways forward and backward. The metal chains on the swing creak to life and wail into the emptiness of the night. She comes to a stop and wraps her arms around herself to rub some warmth into her body.

Shivering, she makes her way downtown. Her lips are falling blue, and snot goes frozen on her face. She passes one closed storefront after another and then stops momentarily at an empty alley, before taking a seat in the snow behind a dumpster. Her eyes close. Her body continues to react to the cold.

Bright headlights of an approaching car cut into the alley, catching her attention. She opens her eyes, gets to her feet, and walks out onto the sidewalk. Cautiously, she steps to the edge of the curb and takes a deep breath. The headlights on the car grow as it barrels down toward her miniature cliff side. She dips one foot over the street as if she were testing the temperature of water, building up the nerve to splash into the unknown. She squeezes her eyes closed tight, raises her arms wide, and steps one foot onto the road. However, the second foot never follows. It hovers, frozen by the sounds of a song coming from somewhere in the distance. She steps back onto the sidewalk. The car whips by furiously, barely missing her.

After regaining composure, her ears follow the tune across the street to Rebels, a dive bar stuck in another decade. An observation only made more apparent by the businesses on either side of it. One, a juice bar called Turmeric & Time. The other, a cell phone store with large LED optical screens as windows that play ads for the newest models, even when the store is closed.

Peter, Paul and Mary's "Leaving on a Jet Plane" hums out from behind the dirty sign hanging above the entrance; backlit and shining a dingy yellow onto the snow-covered sidewalk below. The song spills out louder as a man stumbles through the exit to light a cigarette.

Laura pushes the heavy front door and lets herself in. The regulars look her over with doubtful eyes. Some recognize her, some don't; a few examine her uncommon presence in a place like Rebels. A couple of men continue to stare at her while others quickly focus back on the bottom of their own drinks.

Hurrying past them, mumbling a little "excuse me" she moves to the old jukebox belting out the tune that caught her attention. She stares at the song label behind the dirty glass display and mouths a few lyrics silently. Her eyes close and she clutches her chest. It isn't long before warm tears are trailing down her cheeks. She jolts back to life and wipes her eyes, then takes a seat at the bar. "One bud, please," she says.

The scraggly, leather-faced bartender nods, pulls a fresh one from a bucket of ice, and hands it to her.

"Thank you." Laura downs a few breathless gulps. The fizz settles in her stomach.

"Who chose that song?" she asks the bartender.

He points behind her to a man sitting with an older man; the two of them sharing a laugh over their drinks. The younger man's bright green sweater gives him away. It's the man from the funeral; the onlooker who caught her attention.

Laura's stare causes the younger man to look over. She averts her eyes down to her hand to find her beer, finishes it in one swig, and marches to his table, disregarding any usual pleasantries.

"Why'd you pick that song?"

The man sits up, his soft brown, confused eyes squint at her abrupt question.

"It's a good song," he admits, looking over to his friend for confirmation.

"Great song," the older man says from under a thick, white mustache that matches his unkempt, frazzled hair.

She stares at the younger man, unsure of what to do next.

"Would you like to join me?" the young man asks, filling the silence.

"You can have my chair if you want," says the older man. He hops off the chair and stumbles a bit to catch his balance. She nods a "thank you" and settles into the seat.

"Good night, Martin," the young man says.

The old drunk leans on the table, and whispers, "What did I tell ya, kid? The people that like me call me..."

Together, in unison, they say, "Moo."

"Well, good night, Moo," the young man chuckles.

Moo tips an invisible hat and raises his glass, sipping from it as he walks away. When he is out of sight, the young man places his eyes on Laura, trying to smile.

"That was my son's favorite song," Laura admits, almost as if she were telling it to herself. "He died. You were there...and now you're here, playing the same song. Keeping me from..."

"What am I keeping you from, exactly?"

The question breaks her from her spell. Unsettled, she looks around the bar and lets out a deep helpless breath. She notices his glass is empty and waves down the bartender. "Two whiskeys, please."

"No whiskey. Coca-Cola is fine," the man says.

Confused, Laura asks, "You come to a place like this for a glass of coke?"

"I come to a place like this for many things. One, being that song. It reminds me of someone."

He is a softer-spoken man, for the most part. A bit guarded, with an occasional splash of awkward pause between his thoughts, as if he wasn't fully sure of how to proceed with the conversation.

The bartender places their drinks down. The glasses are that sturdy, been-to-war-and-survived kind, with a few welcoming hints of grime. Laura hands him some cash, fakes a smile, and tells him to keep the change.

"Your son, how did he die?" the man asks.

Laura stiffens at the question.

"I apologize. That was too forward of me"

"No, it's fine. I mean, that's why I'm here. Was my fault. I wasn't paying attention and...he was just being a little kid at the wrong time."

"I'm sorry for your loss."

"I just wish I could hold him again, you know? Feel the warmth and love in his little body. I sit, most nights, in his favorite swing at the playground. Sometimes I think I can hear him in the wind. But I know I'm lying to myself. It's just wind. And there's no more holding him or hearing him." Laura inhales to swallow the tears and then takes a quick swig of her drink. "Enough about that, though. I'm Laura by the way. I'm curious, how come I've never seen you in town since, I don't know, ever?" she asks.

"I don't get back much. That was actually my first day in town," he confesses.

"Here long?"

"I don't plan to be."

"Plans can change, Mr...," she says, hinting at him to finish the sentence.

"Foster. Ellis Foster."

"Ellis," says Laura, testing the name out for the first time.

He smirks and takes a sip of his drink, then professes, "Suddenly, one day, you realize home doesn't always remain in the same place. To me, Hollow Hills is full of ghosts fading behind the sights and sounds of strangers. Out here, it's nothing but cold wind blowing through a land of broken dreams. Look around."

The two of them scan the bar. Three men argue a bit too loudly over football. Beside them is another man, alone, babying a beer. He picks at the label with his finger, staring off into nothing. A white-haired woman sits at the end of the bar, with her back against the wall. She stirs a martini in her hand. Moo sits at a table by himself. He begins falling asleep in his own chest. The only other patron is another older man, large in stature, who sips away at his beer, occasionally talking to himself.

"A collection of hearts as broken as the dreams. I only come back because I have to, not because I want to," Ellis says.

Laura is struck by his honesty. "I was going to kill myself tonight. And Peter, Paul and fucking Mary saved my life," she blurts out. The words work from her brain to her mouth so instinctively, she shocks herself when they make contact with her ears.

"There is power in pain and tragedy," Ellis says, making an effort to be reassuring. "A certain magic in the beauty born from the colors of suffering."

She agrees and lifts her glass. He follows suit.

"Cheers."

Their glasses clank and they drift into conversation as the songs and drunks change around them.

"Who was that man you were talking to?"

"Someone I've run into a few times, but we never really got a chance to talk until now," Ellis says.

"I hope I didn't interrupt anything."

"You did, but that's okay."

Laura laughs.

"It really is okay. When I'm back here, I'm always focused on my job, I guess you could say. That man, unbeknownst to him, was a part of that job. But now you're sitting there, because that song played when you needed it. That seems more important than my conversation with Martin."

"Moo," Laura corrects.

"Yes, Moo." Ellis says.

"So, what's your job? Am I being interviewed?" Laura asks, playfully.

"Hard to explain. I'm a bit of an environmentalist. A de facto dendrologist, in some ways."

"You say that like everyone knows what the fuck dendrologist means."

Ellis laughs. "The science of wooded plants. Dendrology. In my case, I work with one particular type of tree. It's my job to make sure it survives."

"How does one do that? And why would you need an old drunk to help you?"

"I'm not sure you'd believe me without seeing it for yourself."

"Mysterious," Laura jokes.

"Last call!" The bartender shouts as the lights go bright in the bar.

"What side of town do you stay on?" Laura asks.

"I live in the woods."

Laura can't help but giggle. The stoned look on Ellis's face suggests he isn't kidding. She presses him about it. "What do you mean 'In the woods'? Is that a house? A cabin? A tent?"

"How about I show you?"

Laura is jarred by the question, almost insulted he'd have the audacity to invite her back to his place.

"No, please, it's not like that. I mean, you're great and pretty and all, but I'm not, you know, trying to…the tree stuff. My job. I live nearby…," he tries to form the right words, completely flustered. Laura is slightly amused by his discomfort.

The larger man mumbling to himself at the other side of the bar screams, "You're him!" His loud voice turns every head in the small bar. He stands, staring at Ellis with an intense ferocity, and walks over in their direction. "Yeah, you're the magic man...call the cops! He tried to kill me. At the Wayward," stutters the man, maniacally.

"That's enough, Jay," the bartender yells, quite unbothered by the man's comment. Jay stares daggers through Ellis. Ellis doesn't say a word. Jay resigns the tension in his bones and turns to Laura. "Don't go poof, lady," he says, before meandering toward the bar.

Laura, playfully confused, "You're not a cult leader, or a serial killer or some shit, right?"

"Like I would tell you if I was," Ellis replies through laughter.

Laura doesn't appear sure how to react to that.

Ellis grows serious, "This is going to sound crazy. If you decide to trust me right now and come with me. To trust the song. To pull on that same instinct that helped you stick around tonight. To trust THIS moment. I think I can help you, but I can't tell you how. You won't believe me. I have to show you."

Laura searches for the truth in Ellis's eyes.

"The fuck do I have to lose? Lead the way, Dr. Tree."

Finish the Job

❧

Winter 1950

*A*midst the melting pockets of snow, a fawn laps up water from a break in the ice of a stream. Its antlers have barely broken through its skull and the fatigue of a long winter eats away at the innocence of its eyes. Nearby, its father forages for food, paving his way around the deadened brush and barren grounds. Something stirs in the distance.

A gunshot rings out! The stag's head darts up from the ground. A trail of blood leads into the thicket from where the fawn once was. Another shot! Before the stag can respond, the bullet enters and exits its neck, dropping the animal immediately.

Out of the white blanket, Michael and Ellis reveal themselves, long pointed rifles over their shoulders. They approach the dying deer and stand over its body, predators examining their prey. With a swift slide of his blade, Michael slits the stag's throat, ending its misery. He's stoic in the moment, bundled up in a heavy wool coat and pants with pockets weighed down from other weapons and utilities. Patches of his beard poke through the holes of a tattered scarf around his face. A hunting cap with checkered flaps covers his ears. He wipes the knife clean along his pant leg and looks to Ellis, who is staring at the blood leading away from them into the woods. Michael removes the scarf from in front of his mouth. He subtly commands, "Track it."

Ellis, covered in a similar fashion to his father, hesitates.

"Finish the job," his father says, more stern in his demand.

Ellis moves guardedly through the woods; his gun, too big for his body, keeps slipping off his shoulder. The red blots pull him far enough away that the faint ripple from the stream has vanished completely. He stops to allow himself a minute to breathe and study the ground around him. Tiny hoof prints and blood continue a few feet away. Hesitantly, his feet follow the carnage into an opening.

A single, massive oak tree stands dead center. His eyes arouse at the sight of it. The trunk is as wide as three of the largest nearby trees, with thick, scaly bark and a handful of large, knotted roots slightly breaching the dirt at its base. Branches, covered in slow dripping icicles, reach up to touch the sky and fan out to a radius covering half of the clearing. Ellis continues forward until the drops of blood and footprints suddenly stop in the snow before the tree. He searches the ground around the roots. There are no signs of where the deer could have gone.

The Colors of Grief

Winter 2031

*L*aura and Ellis walk toward the edge of town, where the quiet air is eerie and the darkness is endless, save for the moonlight. They keep north, along a rural road, and cross a park-and-ride on Western Pass, breaching a tree line into a wooded cluster. Laura pauses a few feet into the dead brush. "It's not too far," Ellis reassures her. He extends his hand to help.

Laura shivers as her breath turns white in the air. The snow crunches under their feet as they move down a path that leads to the shoreline of a stream. They amble along the water, deeper into the woods.

"Your boss can't really be making you live out here. That's gotta be illegal or something."

In stride he replies, "I sort of have no choice."

The ground opens to the lonesome but imposing oak tree that

makes its home in the clearing. As tall as ever, with the same mangled roots snaking through the dirt and overhang of ominous branches, it swallows Laura's attention.

"Laura, meet JoJo," Ellis says.

He approaches the tree and places his hand on the bark just above a set of initials carved into it: *C.A. + J.L. 5/13/57.*

A void, blacker than the night itself, grows around his hand. It stretches down to where the trunk meets the snow and upward along every branch, illuminating them in deep, neon purple. Laura's feet take a couple unconscious steps back. Her eyes climb the tree and sparkle under the weight of disbelief. Ellis folds his arms and waits, allowing her to savor the moment.

Laura's gaze deviates from the spectacle of the tree to Ellis. "Wha...What's a JoJo?"

"A name a kid gave a magical tree he can't escape," he snickers. "Join me." Ellis steps forward, disappearing into the darkness of the tree.

Laura remains alone in the stillness of the night. She tries to scream "Ellis", but it exits in a whisper. Noises of unseen nature and hidden wildlife heighten in the darkness around her.

"Ellis," she howls.

Only the wind responds.

The pitch-black entrance, highlighted under the luminescence of the branches above it, entices her. Her curiosity pulls on her desperation. She inches her way up to the tree and peers through the black doorway, examining it for clues of anything on the other side. Her eyes only met with more darkness. She enters the void.

The doorway closes behind her with a transparent film; a window, which allows her to see out into the woods she left behind. In front of her, a throbbing blot of red levitates in the distance. Carefully, she advances toward the crimson light. It is dim and small, growing only slightly in her approach. Closer, she recognizes it: a beating heart.

About the size of a tomato, it floats in the black without a body.

"Ellis!"

The heart reacts. Laura quietens. It moves in her direction. Her feet creep forward. Closer now, she sees that it does have a body. One as black as the void; its skin translucent like that of the doorway she stepped through.

The surreal figure is at her feet, and she can clearly see that it is a small deer. It looks up with eyes smooth as glass. She kneels and reaches her hand out to pet it. As her palm touches its head, she is met with an electric shock. Her instincts retract her hand, but her wonder brings it back for another feel. The electric current settles in her; the horror on her face speaks to the hauntings her mind is returned to. She weeps and before she can wipe her face, a few tears grace the black ground around her, causing it to illuminate and ripple. Blue. Purple. Green. Neon and bright; the floor comes to life with the touch of her grief.

"Ellis," she calls once more. A dusting of scattered hues, like a powder, travels from her mouth as she speaks. The particles encompass her.

Ellis's voice emerges from behind her. "Bullet won't hurt you. He's kind and watches over JoJo when I'm not here," he says, emerging from the gloom in front of her.

Laura lingers on the colors.

"Reach out, touch them," Ellis encourages her.

She does. A small apple tree within JoJo comes to life, the purple filling its trunk and limbs as it breathes. A tiny exoskeleton of a boy, caught somewhere between here and not here, steps out of the apple tree. It shapes and shifts itself into a tiny body. The boy removes an apple from a branch. Laura rises, her hand over her mouth, the air in her lungs crashing through her fingers. "Bubs," she murmurs under her breath.

The boy approaches and holds out the apple to his mother.

Ellis interjects and snatches the apple from the boy's palm. Laura reacts unassured.

"Trust me, you don't want to eat this. Now, take the colors and touch him," Ellis instructs.

Conflicted emotions are at war on her face. "Am I dead?"

"No. Please, do it."

She approaches the shadow of her son, scooping from the exotic streams at their feet. Crouched before him with a palm full of blazing red, she reaches for her son's hand. The blush takes to him like paint to a canvas, soaking into his flesh. Another color, and another, and another, Laura continues. "Am I dreaming?" she whispers to herself. Then, proceeds to fill Billy in until he is an abstract painting of himself.

"Mommy," he utters, without using his lips, speaking directly to her mind. Instinct collapses her to her knees. She hugs him, repeating his name over and over. The blackness around them succumbs to the colors. Laura watches the landscapes morph into watercolor paintings, unable to shake the surreal nature of this conscious dreamscape in the sidewalk cracks of reality. Tenderly, she holds Billy's face in her palms, awestruck that he is there.

"What is this place?"

Into the Void

Winter 1950

*C*onfounded with the tree, ten-year-old Ellis hesitates to look around for the fawn any longer. Its branches turn black and the darkness bleeds down along the bark to the ground. The air swirls around the boy, acknowledging his presence. The trunk transforms into a hollow opening. From it, the deer pokes its head out, the tarpit of its eyes lassoing the young boy's determination into the tree.

Inside, scattered drops of blood have changed into a vibrant yellow that creates a path from Ellis's feet to those of the fawn. Ellis follows the trail. The animal, however, grows weak and collapses to the blackened ground. Ellis drops his gun and rushes to the animal's side. He reaches out his tiny hand to pet it. The deer retracts, but soon eases back into the calm hand of death to accept its murderer's compassion.

Ellis caresses the deer's head as it fades away. A tear falls from his face and mixes with the yellow blood. Something shifts within him. His body recoils. The deer's life overcomes the boy's mind in violent flashes that project around them in the void - it breaching its mother's womb, gaining stability on its newborn legs, life grazing in the woods with its father, the bullet ripping through its flesh and, finally, its last breath.

The hole in the tree closes behind them. Ellis releases the fawn's head and hurries to the doorway. He bumps into the crystalline cover stretched across it. Curiously, he taps the window. A movement at the edge of the clearing draws his eyes. His father pushes through the brush, following the same trail of blood he did. Michael spots the footprints in the snow leading to the tree. He walks all the way up to the base of the trunk, turning his glance everywhere for a clue, unable to see Ellis on the other side.

Ellis bangs his fists against the see-through wall, calling out for his father. To his surprise, each scream bursts a colorful cloud of breath from his mouth. He bangs and bangs. Each slam reverberates through the void, trembling the yellow pools of blood across the floor.

His father steps back from the tree and moves on in search of him. Ellis cries harder. He wipes his eyes with his hands and punches at the wall, angrily this time. Each hit is another stain of neon color from where his tears lie wet upon his fists. Exhaling hard to catch his breath, he turns his back to the sealed exit, slides to a seated position clutching his knees, and drops his head into his arms.

Shortly thereafter, there's a nudge on his shoulder. He unfurls the tension in his bones enough to lift his head from his arms and, there, stands the deer, but different - seemingly unreal. Outlined in black and purple, its heart visible and beating inside its body.

Beyond the deer, and all around, there is not a single bit of darkness left. Every bit of black, except for the deer, has been overtaken by the colors of Ellis's sadness. The two of them make eye contact and Ellis manages to find his voice.

36

"Why did you bring me here?"

The fawn stares back, unresponsive. Ellis returns to quietly observing their ornate prison. Dead center, a small tree uproots from the colors. Multicolored apples hang from its neon branches.

Same But Different

Winter 1967

*E*llis hasn't grown an inch or aged a day since entering the tree. However, on the outside, the seasons continue to change. Ellis and the deer, which he's come to name Bullet, watch the snow melt, spring come to life, leaves turn to rust, and the very same snow return, over and over and over. He's lost count of how long he's been trapped within these complexions of his own sadness.

Ellis realized early on that the colors came when he was sad. Years of tears and grief adapting to his situation gave him more to create with. What once started as sketches of a child's imagination, eventually, became paintings worthy of museums. Purple gardens, rainbow lakes, neon mountains, and expansive golden fields stretched as far as the eye could see. The only fixture of this place is the curious little tree-within-a-tree. Early on, even though he never has an appetite, Ellis tries to eat one of the apples from it, but his body rejects it.

The only thing that ever changed within was the loss of light and color. Not all at once but, slowly, over time. The apples began to rot. The colors he cried into existence withered into dull grays and encroaching blacks. The vibrancy faded. Eventually, he came to accept this hidden void as his home. There wasn't an ounce of sadness left to design with. Not a single tear to shed. He had no more pain to give, only boredom.

So, the dark kept returning, and one morning it was all that there was for Ellis and Bullet. Emptiness with no end. A blank canvas the color of night. A tomb. And, one day in early winter, with the last faded breath of color gone and no more sadness left to give the void, the doorway opens as easily as it had closed the day they entered.

Ellis wrestles free from a brief moment of shock and runs for the exit without looking back. The outside air is medicine to his lungs as he inhales like some undiscovered beast. The sound of dead leaves crunching beneath his feet amplifies his determination. His little legs work ferociously through the woods, beyond the stream where he and his father laid in wait to hunt, out onto the street, and into town. He races down streets with familiar names and unfamiliar surroundings. Fewer trees line them. More houses in their place. The cars were strange shapes. The people dressed in ways Ellis didn't recognize.

Whipping around one corner, he tramples through a small group of teenagers, all holding signs and chanting something in unison. Their pants started thin at the waist and got bigger at the bottom, covering their shoes. Some wear face paint of strange symbols and words like "Peace".

He doesn't let up and keeps running down main street, bobbing and weaving through the bodies on the sidewalk. Into the quieter streets, he chugs by house after house, until he screeches to a stop in front of a bright blue one. Catching his breath on the sidewalk, he stares at branches from a tree in the backyard. They are breaching the morning sky above the roof. Through the front gate and up the walkway, a neatly cut lawn surrounds him. Sundials and ornaments and a rock garden sit in organized fashion. He sidesteps a small garden and sneaks around the side of the house to peer over a locked gate. He inspects the large tree in the backyard with a confused look on his face. Back around front, he rings the doorbell. The sound of the door unlocking perks him up, but when it opens, a brown-skinned teenage girl, standing in her pajamas, greets him. His bewilderment deepens.

"Hi there. Can I help you with something?" Her voice is kind. Ellis doesn't respond. He bobs his head side-to-side to get a glance into the house. It is clean and tidy. The walls, beige and spotless. The floorboards are new. The fireplace has pictures of a family that isn't his on the mantle.

"Mom!" The girl turns her attention toward the living room. When the mother arrives, Ellis is gone.

He hurries downtown to Johnny's, but it is no longer Johnny's.

"R-E-B-E-L-S," Ellis spells out the word. Each letter careens him deeper into conundrum. He struggles with the door. Inside, a handful of men sit apart from one another with their drinks. None pay Ellis any mind. "Anyone's kid?" the man behind the bar asks the room. They all look towards the door and then return to their drinks once they see it's not their responsibility. "Can I help you, son?" the burly bartender asks, mustering as kind a tone as he can for a kid.

"Where is Marilyn?" The words shake from the boy's weary voice.

"This some kind of joke, kid?"

Ellis nervously mutters, "N...no..."

The bartender scratches his head. "Kid, my mom died in 1962. Now get."

"But..."

"I said, get!"

Ellis jumps in his tracks and runs away.

He traipses through town to pass the time. Storefronts are

freshly painted. Some with new names. Some with old. People are cleaner and busier. More suits and ties than before. He stops at the playground. It looks similar, but the slide is much bigger. The swing set had double the swings, and there was a giant web of rope that children were climbing to see who could get to the top first. Among all the busy, chattering voices of parents and children, Ellis sits in an empty swing. Timidly, he pushes on the ground with his toes to rock back and forth.

"You gotta get a good push," the girl in the swing next to him yells. A hefty, dirty-blonde boy pushes her higher. Ellis watches them.

"Give him a push, Moo," she instructs the boy.

Moo moves behind Ellis and grabs the chains of his swing, pulling him back. Ellis lifts his feet. The boy pushes him forward. Ellis extends his legs on lift-off and pulls back on descent, to build momentum. The air hugs his body with each new push higher into the air, until there is nothing but blue sky in front of him. Ellis, enraptured, loses track of how high he is.

"Woah!" exclaims Moo. It breaks Ellis from his trance.

Surprised at the distance between him and the ground, his tiny body hurdles from the swing and comes crashing down with a thud. He cringes in pain. A nearby father hurries to his side. "Okay there, pal?" the father asks.

The father turns to Moo, angry. "Martin, how high were you pushing?"

"I didn't do it, Dad," Moo shouts back, apologetically.

Ellis backs away.

"Where are your parents?" the man asks.

Ellis zips to his feet and runs off, pausing to catch his breath in a neighboring alley. He examines himself for bruises or cuts and dusts off mud from his pants. Then, he continues south toward the waterfront. He enters the docks but, like everything else, it is different. Much quieter. Fewer pallets. Even fewer men dragging boxes from one place to another. The only thing there were more of were boats, and they weren't company owned. Names like *The Old Alley* and *Betty Boop* and *Lizard King* adorned their slow-rocking bodies.

The setting sun burns pink across the sky and gusts of wind begin to pick up off the water. Ellis buttons his coat and wraps his scarf around his face. His stomach grumbles. A few dockworkers taking a smoke break notice him.

"Ain't no place for a kid. Buzz off," one of them shouts.

Afraid, Ellis leaves. Back at Rebels, he sneaks around to the rear exit. The door is unlocked. He enters quietly and crouches, stealthily making his way to a counter to snatch a loaf of bread. Then, he opens the refrigerator door and grabs a hunk of cheese. A voice emerges through the kitchen doors from the bar area. "Hey, Tommy, thought I told you to make sure the fridge door is closed all the way."

The bartender closes the refrigerator door and behind it, Ellis clutches his goods, terrified. The man recognizes him from earlier and opens the refrigerator back up to grab a few slices of ham and a small jar of mustard. He extends his hand, offering them to Ellis. "Go on, take it. But don't ever do this again, you hear?"

Ellis agrees, takes the supplies, and exits before the man has a chance to change his mind. With nowhere to stay, he makes his way back to the docks, into a garage where they store some boats for winter. Tucked into the farthest corner of the storage unit is one with no name. It's on a lift. The hull is sanded down and covered in gray primer.

It is musty and dank inside. Cobwebs collect in corners. Nothing much but fishing gear and netting strewn about. A small, brown couch sits along one side of the boat with a cooler on the floor in front of it. The floor creaks under his weight as he goes to sit. He places the food down on top of the cooler, then digs through the gear and finds a mess kit. He removes a small metal plate and puts it down on the cooler. With the knife from the kit, he slices the bread in half lengthwise and sets it down on the plate. The sound of the mustard jar popping open excites him. He shovels out a giant glob with the knife and slathers it until there isn't a single uncovered grain of bread. The ham gets placed evenly. Then, he slices the cheese and puts it atop the ham, three slices long. The sandwich is the size of his head. His mouth waters at the sight of it; his eyes already eating it before his stomach has a chance to. He raises it to his face and, like a wild animal, tears into it. A deep, satisfied moan fights its way out of his mouth between chews.

Completely stuffed and tired, he fashions some of the netting into a makeshift blanket and lies down on the couch. Surrounding sounds keep him up most of the night, until his eyes can no longer hold themselves open.

***

The following morning, he wakes to an odd scratching sound outside. He steps out and sticks his head over the side of the boat. A worker kneels below, sanding the hull, with a thermos and a newspaper on the ground by his feet. Ellis ducks out of sight and hides below deck. He waits a few hours for the sound to stop and then gives it another go.

This time, the worker is gone. Ellis climbs down the lift and hops off, tumbling face first to the ground. He pushes himself up, realizing he landed on the worker's newspaper. The date nestled into the top corner of the front page reads: *November 15th, 1967.*

***

The bartender at Rebels gets the joint operational for the day. He lowers the chairs from the tables, wipes down the bar top, and changes the urinal cakes. Upon exiting the bathroom, Ellis is standing in the vestibule of the bar entrance with the newspaper in his hand.

"Kid, what did I tell ya?"

The man goes behind the bar to keep working, sorting glasses, and replacing empty liquor bottles on the shelves. Ellis remains at a standstill in the doorway. His eyes follow every movement the bartender makes. The bartender tries to ignore the boy's presence but can't. He places the vodka bottle in his hand down with some force and turns toward Ellis.

"If you're not gonna leave, you better get talking then."

Ellis walks over to the bar, his head just meeting the height of the counter, and places the newspaper down in front of the man. "Is that the real date?" Ellis stutters.

The man's brows contract from the bizarre question. "What do you mean? What other date would it be? Yeah, it's real." The man's voice resounds within the closed bar.

Ellis moves his gaze to the ground, clutching onto the newspaper tighter.

"Kid, you need help?"

Ellis climbs on top of a stool to face the man. "My pa, do you know him? He knew Marilyn."

The bartender's confusion only grows.

"Your dad knew my mom?"

Ellis shakes his head.

"Okay, I'll play along. What's your dad's name?"

"Michael Foster."

"Foster?" The man questions. "I remember that name from when I was a kid. Whole town looking for a boy. My mother putting up fliers. That poor man dying without an answer."

Ellis's posture slumps and air slowly leaves his tiny body.

"My pa...My pa is dead?" The boy's eyes recede.

"Michael Foster did die, yes. But ain't no way he could be your pa. You okay, kid?"

Ellis looks to the ground without saying anything.

"You wait right there and I'm gonna get you some help, kid."

The bartender pulls a rotary phone from under the bar and places it on the counter. He picks up the receiver and begins to swing the dial with the end of his pointer finger, one number at a time. Ellis backs away from the bar.

"Hold tight, kid"

Ellis darts out the door and gets lost amongst the people in town, leaving the flummoxed bartender with several questions lingering in his eyes.

St. Marie

Winter 1967

A modest, marble tombstone in a nondescript row of the Hollow Hills Cemetery displays a simple plaque with the etching: *Michael D. Foster (September 21, 1906 – September 18, 1954)*

Ellis surrenders to his grief and mourns his father. He wipes the tears from his face and studies them on his fingers. No fantastical colors. No signs of that place. Only water and salt. Eventually, his eyes give all they can, and he sits in the silence of the graveyard.

An older woman, in a knitted blue sweater, with a scarf around her wrinkled neck, approaches a grave a few plots away. The headstone, cleaner than his father's, reads: *James A. Perry (April 12, 1901 - March 2, 1964)*

The woman kneels and makes the sign of the cross with her hand. Ellis watches as she pulls a rosary from her pocket and spins the beads with her trembling fingers to recite a prayer. Upon finishing, she drapes the rosary over the top of the grave, then gently rests her palm on the bare marble and whispers a few words to herself. The woman brings her hand to her mouth, kisses it, plants it on the gravestone, and administers one last sign of the cross.

Back to her feet, she brushes the dirt off her knees and notices Ellis staring. The dirt on his face, his tattered coat, and messy hair draws her closer. She towers over him as he sits cross-legged. "Lovely day for them to have visitors," she suggests. Her sorrowful green eyes disarm the tension in Ellis. He stands up. Closer now, she kneels to match his height. "My name is Marie. What's yours, sweetheart?"

"Ellis."

A smile breaks on her face. She looks at the grave he's standing at and reads it. "Michael Foster. Your Grandfather?"

"My father."

A befuddled look flares up on her face. She scans the date once more. "How old are you, Ellis?"

He counts to himself using his fingers. His soft brown eyes stare directly into Marie's. "I..., umm, I think...twenty-seven," he says.

"Well, where does a grown man such as yourself live?"

"The woods for a long time, but now I live in a boat at the docks," Ellis exclaims.

Marie stands, taking a moment to herself.

To the grave she visited, she whispers, "James, what do I do?"

Back facing Ellis, she is met with his pitiful, puppy dog eyes.

"Okay, sweetie." Marie kneels again to fix his coat. "I need you to trust me and come with me. My car is that white one right over there." Marie points to an Oldsmobile parked at the end of the row of graves. "We can take it into town and get some help."

Ellis looks at the car. It's big and shiny. The hood stretches across most of it. The tires have clean, white circles on them. A crucifix big enough to see from where they stand dangles from the mirror over the dashboard. "C'mon," she says.

With extreme caution, he walks with her. Marie digs a granola bar out of her pocket. "Here, you must be famished. Eat this."

***

Chubby Checker's "The Hucklebuck" plays low on the radio. Marie hums along, moving her shoulders, and tapping with her fingers on the steering wheel. "We loved this song. James and I. We were quite a pair back in the day. The dance floor didn't stand a chance."

Buckled in tight and chewing on the granola bar, Ellis asks, "Who is James?"

"My husband. That's who I was visiting. I come here once a week to see him." Her smile grows at the thought.

"How did he die?"

Marie's smile falters. "Well, he got sick a few years ago and, to put it simply, none of the medicine worked."

"I'm sorry." Ellis lowers the music. "Can you tell me how my pa died?"

Marie slows the car and comes to a stop in town. She turns to face Ellis. "You promise you aren't messing with an old lady?"

"I'm not," he replies earnestly.

Marie picks up speed again. A short distance down main street she parks at a corner where a phone booth stands. She unbuckles her seatbelt. "Stay here, sweetheart."

"Where are you going?" he asks.

"I need to make a quick phone call. I'll be back in a moment. I promise," she says and gets out.

Marie comes around the front of the car and enters the booth, promptly flipping through the phone book. Her pointer finger slides down a list of names beginning with F. There are no listings for Foster. Next, she thumbs through the pages for the police station and dials.

A man answers. "Hollow Hills P.D., Deputy Woodrow, is this an emergency?"

"Hello, officer. A bit of an odd question for you, but have

there been any recent reports of a missing boy?" Marie inquires.

"Hold on, ma'am."

Marie holds the phone tightly to her ear as she fixes her attention on the car. Ellis stares in her direction. She winks and gives him a thumbs up.

"Thank you for holding, ma'am. Can you please describe the boy in question?" the deputy asks.

"Umm, yes. Ten to twelve years old. Thin. A bit malnourished, if I'm being honest. Brown eyes. Brown hair."

"Well, ma'am, nothing fitting that description has been filed. Do you want to file a report?"

"What about anything for the name Foster, Michael, or Ellis?" she asks, completely ignoring his question.

"Ma'am, can you let me know what you need exactly?"

"Officer, it's urgent and quite important. I'm trying to find a relative," she emphasizes.

"Alright. Please hold for me, again," he says, a sense of duty in his voice.

Marie sits on hold for several minutes. Ellis continues to watch from the car. She smiles for him.

"Ma'am, are you still there?"

"Yes, officer," Marie perks up.

"According to records, there are no apprehensions with that name. Only an old file for the name Foster, a Michael David Foster," the deputy says, a slight pause in conversation as he rustles through more papers, "Seems like he actually filed a missing person's report for his son back in the winter of 1950. Ellis. Is there something you know about this case, ma'am?" his tone shifts, concerned.

Marie lowers the phone from her ear, in awe. The deputy repeats "Ma'am" over and over, until she finally hangs up. Clutching the crucifix around her neck, with her eyes to the sky, "How, James? How?"

She exits the phone booth and collects herself before getting back in the car. Ellis eagerly sits with the same lost look as before. She buckles her seatbelt without a word.

"Did you find out about my pa?"

She starts the car.

"Not quite, honey. But I will. In the meantime, I have an idea."

***

Ellis exits a fitting room in a boutique. He looks slick in tailored brown slacks and a dark green sweater. His head bent into his chest, he runs a hand through the soft fabric, admiring the beautiful threading. Marie adjusts his body to face the mirror in the store.

"So handsome. Green is your color."

The two of them share a smile in the mirror. Marie works her fingers in his hair, fixing it into a tidy part. "Do you like it?"

"I love it," says Ellis. His eyes gleam in the mirror.

Marie collects a neat pile of clothes off a chair and brings them to the cash register. Ellis grabs her free hand, stopping her in her tracks. She looks down to his tiny fingers curled into hers. Then, to his eyes, aglow in warmth.

***

Marie pulls into the driveway of a white, two-story house with a red-brick chimney. The front porch is occupied by two wicker chairs. There are stained glass ornaments hanging in front of them, bristling in the wind. A bare birch tree stands at the corner of a small garden, its branches hanging from the sky in similar fashion to the one Ellis left behind.

Inside, the first thing Ellis notices are bookshelves in a study right off the foyer. One wall is head-to-toe and side-to-side with books. On the adjacent wall there are hundreds of records bookending a turntable system.

"Later, we can listen to music. You need to clean up for dinner first," Marie's voice reaches Ellis.

Upstairs, Marie leads him into a spare bedroom. There isn't a sign of clutter or speck of dust in sight. The wallpaper is bright white with flower designs woven throughout. A bed is cozily parked against the center of the far wall, with lamps on either side of it. "Go on," Marie says, "It's yours."

Ellis steps into the room with a smile firmly stretched across his face.

"You make yourself at home and I will draw you a warm bath."

***

Ellis enters the kitchen in pajamas that are a bit loose near his waist. His hair is still wet from the bath. From the corner of the kitchen, he watches Marie stir a pot of tomato sauce. The sight of the food drags him closer to the counter. The aroma creeps up his nostrils and enchants a rumble from his belly.

"Set the table for me, Ellis. What you need is just over there." Marie's head nods to the end of the counter.

Ellis spots two bowls, two plates, two glasses, and utensils. He picks them all up, holding them firm in his hands, focused on not dropping anything. He sets the small, round kitchen table where a tossed salad already awaits. Marie carries the pot of tomato sauce over and places it down on a red trivet. Then, she retrieves a bowl of spaghetti. Lastly, she removes fresh garlic bread from the oven. Ellis sits in anticipation, licking his lips. The sounds of his stomach speak for him as he reaches for the bread, but Marie pulls it away.

"We say Grace in this house. Aren't you Catholic?"

Ellis shrugs his shoulders. Marie sits down across from him with a smile and holds out her hands. Ellis puts his in hers. She closes her eyes. He follows suit. Marie recites Grace, "Bless us, O Lord, and these, thy gifts, which we are about to receive from thy bounty. Through Christ, our Lord. Amen." Her eyes slowly open with delight. Ellis's eyes remain closed. "You say Amen, too," she tells him.

"Amen."

Marie spoons spaghetti into his bowl. His eyes dart open and he snatches a slice of garlic bread from the basket, biting right in. He spends dinner solely focused on eating. Marie decides to break the silence.

"So, what are your hobbies?"

He shrugs.

"Isn't there something you really like to do?"

He considers the thought, "Play with colors."

***

After dinner, the two of them retreat to the study. Marie slides a Fats Domino record off the shelf, unsheathes the vinyl and places it on the player. It spins with a quiet crackle as she moves the needle into position. "Blue Monday" begins. She mumbles a few lyrics in a low hum.

"Why don't you pick a book for yourself, and I'll start a fire," she instructs Ellis.

The bookcase dwarfs him. He moves book by book across the shelves at eye level. Most of the books are aged and worn. Some remain untouched. It doesn't take long for Ellis to choose. He pulls it from the shelf - *The Time Machine*. He goes to the couch and sits beside Marie, who is nestled under a knitted blanket with her own book in her lap. She checks out his book. "Perfect choice."

Ellis pulls another blanket off the arm of the couch and puts it over his lap. The music mixes with the soft hiss of the fire, lulling them deeper into their books. Not before long, a thud startles Marie. She lowers her book to identify the sound. On the floor, by her feet, lies *The Time Machine*. Beside her, Ellis is sound asleep, wrapped in his blanket like a cocoon.

A Moment of Prayer

🍎

Winter 1967

*E*llis wakes to the smell of food. The blinds are wide open. He wears the sunlight on his face. He rubs his eyes to adjust to the light and sits up, realizing he's slept in the study. Burnt logs sleep in the ashes of the fireplace and the record player is shut. *The Time Machine* sits alone on the couch cushion to his left. He steps off the couch. The floor moans beneath him.

"Oh, Ellis. You're up. Come, have some breakfast," Marie shouts from the kitchen.

The table is set with a mountain of pancakes, a warm saucer of syrup, rows of bacon, and a large pitcher of orange juice. "Good morning, dear. Have a seat next to me."

Ellis sits. He then holds out his hands for her with his eyes closed. She laughs. They say Grace and eat.

"Eat up. Growing boys need a big breakfast," she encourages.

Ellis smears butter in between each of his three pancakes. Then, he pours syrup over them, pausing a moment to smell the heavenly maple. He cuts a huge chunk from the stack and shovels it into his mouth, followed by a piece of bacon slathered in the pool of syrup collecting on the plate.

"I made some calls this morning...about your father."

Ellis, with a mouthful of pancakes, stops chewing.

"There's no easy way to do this, Ellis," she says, readjusting in her seat. "Your father fell ill. It was his liver."

"He was a stupid drunk," Ellis spews in anger, avoiding eye contact with Marie.

"I bet he was very sad without you. I bet he was very sad from other things as well. Sometimes, that's why adults drink. They are sad or afraid or lonely. It can make them act mean because they don't know what to do with all those feelings bottled up inside," Marie explains, tender notions in her voice.

"Do you think he missed me?" Ellis's question jumps over the end of her statement.

"Oh, Ellis, of course he did. I bet he never gave up looking for you."

"You can't know that," he fires back.

"You're right. I can't. But I'd like to believe he never gave up."

"Why?"

"Because I know I would never give up if you were my son."

"Maybe you should be my mom then," he declares, excitedly.

"Oh, I'm much too old to be your mom, Ellis," Marie says, a slight chuckle escaping her lips.

"I don't think that matters."

"Then, what does?"

"You make really good food and you would look for me."

Marie can't help but laugh.

"I will think about it, okay?"

"Okay, then, Marie." Ellis continues to eat.

"You know what might be nice of us to do for your father?"

Ellis stares, unsure.

***

St. Sebastian's is fairly empty. A few people kneel in prayer in various pews. A younger priest prepares the altar with wine and eucharist for the next mass. Marie and Ellis stand before a candle rack positioned under the fourth station of the cross, with a small statue of the Virgin Mary atop the rack. Several of the candles are lit.

"Your father never took you to church?" Marie asks.

Ellis shakes his head "no".

"Well, these are votives. You set a prayer of intention for someone else and light it. A lot of the time people do it for those who have already passed."

"Like, for James?"

"Yes, I often say a prayer for James to let him know he isn't alone. I ask the angels to watch over him. I thought, if you're up for it, we could pray for your father."

Ellis stares intently at the flame of one of the candles, then up to the Virgin Mary's eyes.

Marie places her hand on his shoulder. "You can say all the things you want to say to your father that you never got a chance to. You can tell him you're okay and safe. Maybe it will give his spirit peace. What do you say?"

"That might be a nice thing to do, Marie," Ellis says.

"Great. Pick your candle," she instructs.

Ellis scans the rows and settles on one that sits front and center. Marie hands him a candle meant to light the others and he uses it. She takes the same candle to light one directly next to the one Ellis chose. Then, she instructs Ellis to kneel beside her on the platform in front of the rack.

"Take as long as you need. Remember to pull the words from

your heart and speak them to yourself, in your mind. When you're done, say Amen."

Marie does the sign of the cross, clasps her hands, and closes her eyes. Ellis follows suit. The two of them remain in silence, focused on their individual prayers. Shortly after, Marie says, "Amen."

She opens her eyes to find Ellis still focused and doesn't disturb him. Instead, she quietly takes a seat in the nearest pew. Several minutes pass and Ellis doesn't budge. His prayer carries on for several minutes more, until his voice finally cracks, "Amen."

He turns to find Marie in the pew. She waves him over. He goes and takes a seat next to her. "Perfect timing, mass is about to start."

***

Back home, Ellis hurries into the study to pick up where he left off in *The Time Machine*. Several moments later, Marie enters with a small box in her hands. "You said you liked playing with colors," she says, placing the box down in front of Ellis, "I remembered I had these lying around." It's filled with wax crayons of all colors and a white notebook. He's elated.

The two of them spend the rest of the day in the study, alternating between reading, drawing, and listening to vinyl records. Ellis moves his body to the rhythm of the music. They cycle through record after record; Ellis asking about every musician she plays, from The Beatles to The Zombies and Miles Davis.

Deep into the afternoon, while The Mamas and The Papas fill the house, Ellis sits on the floor with crayons spread around him, drawing in the notebook. He is engrossed. Marie sits on the couch, under her blanket, reading *The Spy Who Came in From the Cold* by John le Carré. Ellis's attention trades places between watching her and intently coloring. It isn't long before he is finished. He drops the crayon he's using and observes the drawing one last time. Satisfied, he rips the page from the book and takes it to Marie.

Marie drops her book to her lap. He holds out the paper for her. She takes it from him. It's a drawing of her reading on the couch. Her body is red and yellow, and the floor is covered in blue swirls resembling waves. The wall behind her is a series of fractured shapes of various colors that fit together like a puzzle, reminiscent of the stained-glass ornaments hanging on her front porch. "My goodness! This is beautiful, Ellis. How did you learn to draw like this?"

"I taught myself. In the woods. To cover the darkness. There's color when you cry in the place I was stuck. It's not like out here. When you feel bad in there, it's really pretty," he says, now sitting next to her, "You are sad, Marie. I can tell. You miss James. This is how beautiful I think your sad is."

Marie is speechless. Her eyes shake. Ellis's skinny arms wrap around her. She hugs him back.

Christmas Hymnal

Winter 1967

*C*hristmas Eve arrives. A bunch of red and white flowers sit in a vase upon a table in the study, accompanied by a plate of freshly baked chocolate cookies and a glass of milk. The wood in the fireplace crackles and glows between radiant, gold flames. Two stockings hang from the mantle. A modest, but well decorated tree nestles into a corner of the room, embellished with gold trinkets and glitter. Fake snow and a handful of presents lay underneath it, surrounding a small manger. A record hums Christmas Carols while the two of them read in peace. Marie in her spot on the couch and Ellis sprawled out on the floor, in his pajamas, with pillows and a blanket.

He is nearly finished with *The Time Machine* and can't help but re-read a portion where the narrator concludes: *But, to me, the future is still black and blank – is a vast ignorance, lit at a few casual places by the memory of his story.*

A wave of melancholy rises in Ellis's face. He closes the book and puts it down. Then, he surveys the room. Marie, lost in her own book, smiling occasionally at the words she reads, the dimples in her cheeks coming to life. The music powers on around them in rhythm with the warmth of the swirling fireplace. A home. A family.

Marie places a bookmark on the page she is reading, closes the book, and places it in her lap. She raises her head to look at Ellis, who is trying to form words in his mouth.

"Do you think it's possible to stop time?" he asks.

Marie's eyes look away from Ellis, deep in thought. She crafts her words carefully. "I believe the world is full of all types of mysteries, possibilities, and unanswered questions."

"If you could, would you?" Ellis continues.

Marie purses her lips in reflection.

"No, I don't suppose I would. Life is more than us; it's what's outside moving and growing. I'd feel stuck and I don't see the point in standing still. I'd rather miss the past than have no future."

Lost in his mind and biting his lower lip, Ellis's face depletes its curiosity. A hopeless shadow casts over his eyes as his head lowers to his body.

Marie gets off the couch and joins him on the floor. "But, if I could, think of how special that is, for magic to choose a person. I'd freeze time right now, for you and me."

Ellis smiles, the corner of his eyes crinkling at the thought. Marie checks the time on a clock hanging above the fireplace. It's 11:47 PM "You know, technically, we are supposed to wait until tomorrow for presents, but it's close enough to midnight. What do you say, we sneak one in?"

Ellis is excited.

"Go ahead, pick one," she tells him.

He beelines for a flat square wrapped in red paper, with a green bow.

"That looks like a good one," she says.

He joins her on the couch and tears it open. It's *Album 1700* by Peter, Paul and Mary. His eyes light up.

"You seemed to take a liking to their other records."

"Can I play it now?" he asks.

"Umm, alright, only because it's Christmas," Marie concedes, as Ellis happily proceeds towards the record player. "One song before bedtime. After all, you don't want Santa to pass us by."

Ellis is so ecstatic he accidentally places the needle down on the second song instead of the start of the album. The player makes a warbled scratch to catch up and then begins playing "Leaving on a Jet Plane".

He hurries over to the couch and grabs Marie by the hands, urging her to get up and join him. She gives in, unfolds her legs from the couch and walks to the center of the room with him. Together, they dance. Ellis leans his small head into her stomach. She places her hand in his hair. The ache in the song swallows them as they gently sway about the room.

"I'm sorry I couldn't get you anything for Christmas, Marie." His little voice overflows with disappointment.

"Oh, Ellis, my boy, you've given me more than you'll ever know."

The winter continues in this way. The snow falls and the white winds blow. Ellis ritualistically marks an "X" on the calendar in the kitchen for each new day he wakes up in Marie's house. During the day, she educates him from a stitched together lesson plan reminiscent of her days as a teacher. Occasionally, if the cold lets up, they go out for a walk around Kentwood Park; a sizable stretch of grass connecting the upper rurals to the beginning of main street. Their evenings consisted of reading by the fireplace, him under a blanket on the floor and her, on the couch, swimming in one of James' sweaters. And that was it, their simple routine.

Meeting Magic

———— 🍎 ————

Winter 1967

*I*n the study, Marie finishes up the day's math lesson, while Ellis focuses more on the sunshine outside the window than the equations she rattles off. The branches on the trees have changed, appearing to be free from the clutches of winter. The day is much warmer than when Ellis arrived and there's finally no snow on the ground. Marie doesn't bother to try and keep him focused any longer and shuts her book.

"Finally," Ellis exclaims with a sigh of relief.

Marie feigns disbelief with her mouth agape, "And here I am thinking I'm raising a little gentleman the whole time."

"Sorry, I'm..."

Marie cuts Ellis off. "I know. I'm teasing. Go get ready."

Ellis enters the foyer, shoves his feet into his shoes without using his hands, and grabs his and Marie's coats from where they hang by the front door. He heads back into the study where Marie is rummaging through an end table, removing a few dollars wedged between other junk. Then, she goes to one of the bookshelves and pulls the dictionary, reaching into the empty space for a few more dollars. Ellis watches, perplexed.

"James always said a person should never keep all their money in one place. Can't trust the banks. You know, I still find some of his hiding places all these years later. Coat pockets. Oil cans in the shed. I think he even put some in the foundation out back, but I'm not strong enough to pull out the bricks. Could be a fortune and I'd never know," she tells Ellis. Marie empties change from a mason jar that was tucked behind a stack of records. "I think this will do for snacks."

***

At the park, Ellis and Marie lay out a blanket. The fresh grass pokes around it. The trees are still empty, but the air brushes soft against their bark. Apart from Marie and Ellis, a couple of other people are out enjoying this first fresh breath of changing seasons.

The two of them spend the afternoon playing 500 Rummy, reading in silence, and enjoying the fruit and sandwiches Marie prepared. Ellis cleans up after lunch and proceeds to the garbage cans in the park. He tosses the foil and baggies into the trash, then takes a moment to stare at the sky; a blue wonder. Open and vast, it entrances him. He stares as if it's the first time he's ever seen the sky. A jogger tosses an apple core into the trash can as she passes. It pulls Ellis back to Earth.

He returns to the picnic blanket. Marie fixates on a young couple a short distance away in the grass. The woman sits between her husband's legs, reading *The Clocks* by Agatha Christie. He reads the book over a shoulder he occasionally plants a kiss on.

"Marie?"

She's startled.

"Everything okay?"

"Yes, Ellis. I'm fine."

"Are you sure?"

"It's nothing, sweetie," she says, forcing a subtle smile. "They just remind me of a different time."

"Are they going to get naked?" Ellis asks.

"Stop that, Ellis," Marie demands, not a single ounce of levity in her voice.

"But that's what people in love do. Take off their clothes."

"Enough of it!" Marie snaps. She stands, glaring down at Ellis. "Let's get a move on before we lose the daylight."

He promptly packs their belongings. Marie snatches one last glance at the happy couple before they leave the park.

***

The walk home is shrouded in silence until Ellis finds a stick in the road and uses it as a sword to fight off imaginary foes. At the front gate of the house, Ellis yells, "Marie, move back!" She plays along and steps away from the gate.

"What is it, Ellis?"

"Bridge Trolls! They want to eat us alive," boasts Ellis. He wildly swings his stick.

Marie breaks into laughter, encouraging him, "Take that you evil troll! This is the first and last time you mess with Sir Ellis Foster, hero of the land, and master magician!"

Ellis points his open palm at the gate, pretending to surge a blast of fire at the troll. "Take that!"

"My hero!" Marie shouts. She claps loudly at his victory.

Ellis reaches to open the gate and is struck by a sudden flash of pain throughout his body. He loses balance and falls to his knees. Marie rushes to his side. She holds his tiny, immobilized body in her arms; beads of sweat engulf his face. Marie puts the back of her hand against his forehead. "You're on fire. Let's get you inside," she says, helping him to his feet. They make it a few steps forward and he collapses on the front lawn.

Bedridden, with a severe fever and sharp, unrelenting headaches, he falls in and out of consciousness. The pain comes to him like a wave, sending uncontrollable shivers down his spine and drenching him in cold sweat. Periodically, he opens his eyes. Marie takes his cold palm in hers and rubs his head with her other hand. He is struck with a thunderous flash of pain in his head, escorted by a vision of Bullet dying in the doorway of his bedroom. Ellis tries to speak but is hit, again, with the same anguish and vision - Bullet calling him with pitch-black eyes, the deer's wound bleeding. The agony begins to spread out across Ellis's body in random bursts underneath his skin, setting his insides on fire.

The boy rolls from the bed and falls to the floor. Reeling, he hugs his own body in the fetal position. Marie kneels, trying to calm him. Ellis struggles to maintain a grip on reality as the visions of Bullet last longer with each new crushing blow to his body. The bedroom starts to lose color around the deer. Grays and blacks bleed across the walls. He closes his eyes as hard as he can and screams, "I can't go back!"

Marie tries her best to stop his shaking and covers him with warm blankets. He continues to kick and contort in pain. The hair on his arms starts to grow. He screams in discomfort, fighting to reach his feet. Marie struggles to remove his socks, which are tighter than they should be. Before her very eyes, Ellis's whole body grows. His pajama pants rip and the muscles in his arms tear the tiny shirt off his back. She watches in disbelief as he shrieks in helpless misery over his transformation into the person he should already be.

Now, a young man, Ellis is soaked and trembling as he eases from the pain. He appears rather silly, half naked in the shredded clothing of a ten-year-old boy. With haste, Marie covers him in a blanket, then helps him to the bed. Visions of Bullet blot like sunspots. The deer, fading in and out of his bedroom. The walls, slipping between reality and a colorless landscape.

Marie heads to the bathroom and wets a clean rag with cold water. Upon her return, Ellis has passed out in bed. Digesting what occurred, she sits beside him and wipes his brow with the rag. She turns off the light and takes a seat in the corner of the room to remain close.

Ellis awakens in the middle of the night to yet another jolted vision of the deer, near death, at the door of his room, luring him back. He sits up, his broad arms around his knees, trying not to look at the hologram of the dying creature. He musters enough energy to get to his feet and then quietly passes the sleeping Marie, making sure the faint squeaks of the floor do not wake her.

He moves about the upstairs hallway, into her bedroom. It's immaculate. A brown fur blanket is spread clean over a white bed. A cupboard full of books and framed photos of her and James caddies one corner of the room. Beside it sat a dresser. Ellis rummages through it and takes some of James' clothes. He puts them on and stands before a mirror on the opposite side of the room. What stares back at him is the face and body of a man in his late twenties. Hair was in places it never was before, including a thin layer of scruff sprinkled across his face. It was an alien body with larger limbs and tougher skin, his face resembling his father more than it ever had before.

"Ellis?" Marie's voice calls from his bedroom but, when she enters hers, he is gone.

***

Ellis walks downtown, past the playground, past Rebels, past all the old things he was starting to remember again. On a more desolate road, closer to where the woods begin to line the shoulder, a sudden blast from a car horn frightens him.

"Marie!"

She rolls down the window and growls, "What do you think you're doing?"

A breath he didn't know he was holding in, releases. "That day, I went hunting with my pa."

"What day, Ellis?" Marie asks, puzzled.

"The day I got stuck in JoJo. I don't know why it opened. I think that's why I'm sick. I've been gone too long. I'm catching up to who I'm supposed to be," he says, shivering. "The black and blank ignorance, Marie. It wants me back."

Marie struggles to find the right words. Her sorrowful eyes gleam in the moonlight.

"Time stops in there," he tells her, "I stay the same and everything else changes."

"What are you talking about, sweetie?"

"I don't know how to explain it."

"Then, show me."

"It's too far-"

"Show me, Ellis," Marie interrupts. "I want to know what has happened to you, my poor, sweet boy. Show me your timeless place and your magic. Oh, and before I forget..."

Marie reaches down and holds up his copy of *The Time Machine*.

It's a tough walk for Marie, but Ellis helps her through the woods, beyond the stream, and before the oak tree. There it stands, as fierce as ever, claiming victory over him. Ellis approaches, his eyes stretching from base to peak. It lingers in the darkness like some creature waiting to pounce. He proceeds to place his hand on its bark, over *C.A + J.L. 5/13/57*, which darkens around his palm and opens.

"In here, Marie," he says, stretching out a hand for her. Marie grabs hold and steps in with him.

Bullet's heart beats in the distance of the pitch-black surroundings. Marie grabs Ellis's palm tighter.

"This is JoJo."

"JoJo?" Marie asks.

The heart gets closer until they are practically standing over it.

The deer's form is hardly distinguishable from the black background.

"Marie, this is Bullet. I think what I did to him made me get stuck in this place and it just wanted to send me out to make me sad again. To make me miss the things I can no longer have."

"But why would it do that?" she asks. Tears well in her eyes. A few break free.

He uses his thumb to wipe her cheek and holds out his hand to show her. "Here," he says. The bright purple on his hand stuns Marie.

"See? I told you your sad is really beautiful."

He looks away from Marie and into the darkness.

"I think it gets hungry for our sad. It wants more from me, but I haven't cried in a long time," he says.

With the handful of purple, Ellis constructs a small garden for Marie to sit in. The color takes to the void and rejuvenates Bullet. Ellis shows fewer signs of sickness. He reconstructs his apple tree. "I can't eat them. This place doesn't let me get hungry," he says.

He continues to fill the void with colors. Bullet walks over to the apple tree to greet another figure. A man, perhaps. Marie begins to unsettle. She tries to get to her feet, but her shaky legs don't seem to support her. Ellis lends her a hand off the patchy grass.

"What is it, Marie?" he asks.

Marie is so fixated on the figure that she hardly pays Ellis any mind. She lets out a deep breath, which floats on in rich, green hues. Her hands to her heart, she lets out a whisper. "James."

Holding onto Ellis for support, she stands before James, unable to muster any more words. Her eyes cloud with a swell of emotion. Her hand travels from her chest to her mouth, as if to assist in pulling words from her throat. She slowly lays a hand on James' chest, his body solid against her fingers. He's real. Silent tears turn into loud sobs as she swallows him in a hug, kissing his face and running her hands through what's left of his hair. The colors from her tears fill in his form, rendering him into a pulsing kaleidoscope. "My love."

Ellis happily watches their reconnection as James unlocks from the embrace and plucks a blue apple from the tree. He holds it out to her. She takes it and bites into it. A fire lights in her eyes as the flavors attack her taste buds. "It tastes like all my favorite things at once." Marie delights, sinking her teeth into it with another huge bite.

Then, James holds out his hand for Marie. She gives in. He takes her hand firm in his, pausing for a moment to feel her flesh before turning to the apple tree. Awash in bliss, she follows. James touches a branch on the apple tree and, with a flash, the two of them vanish. The tree-within-a-tree brightens and the roots flicker in a variety of iridescent glows throughout the black below Ellis's feet. Ellis straightens up, swimming in disbelief.

"Marie?!"

His gardens and hills and rivers return around him. He yells for her, again. Nothing. He goes to the apple tree and calls out again. Nothing. She is gone. Swallowed into the void. Gasoline to a churning engine. Fumes.

Furious, Ellis smears the beauty around him, disfiguring and blurring one landscape into another. He punches at the apple tree, each hit splatting along its bright, red bark. The hole he entered closes. He is trapped, once again, in a destiny he never asked for. Bullet sits, casually, on a patch of grass and watches Ellis give in to futile gestures of rage.

Hunger

Winter 2031

*E*llis stands, staring at the apple tree, with his back to Laura and Billy. "In a flash, she was gone. I had no idea why at the time. It took a few trips back out to realize this place, it needed some form of human tragedy to satiate its hunger. That it would starve out eventually and extend my leash to get it fed."

"Do you want to feed me to this place...to JoJo?" Laura asks, with more curiosity than concern.

Ellis turns to face her. "No. Your pain seemed much too fresh. I wanted to feed Moo to it," explains Ellis, "I had a feeling it would show you your son, though. It's always given people the ones they've lost. The souls tightly tethered to their grief."

"But at some point, you'll have to offer someone to it, right?"

"Yes, otherwise I'll get sick and age all the years I haven't been able to live out there."

"How many years has it been?"

"Nearly one hundred, I think."

Billy puts his cold little hand in Laura's. Ellis watches, his eyes soften. "I've spent so long giving this place what it needs for my own selfish reasons. I'm thinking, maybe it's time I use it to give someone else what they need."

Laura deepens in thought, fixed on the vivid patterns of Billy's skin. "Who came out for you, when you first got trapped?"

"That's the sick joke of it all. Nobody."

"I'm sorry, Ellis. I can't begin to imagine what this has been like for you."

Ellis contemplates the moment, but changes directions. "You are free to come and go as you please. JoJo stays open until the equinox."

Laura leans down and plants a kiss on Billy's head. The boy then runs off to splash in the dynamic puddles of iridescence sprinkled about. "What if I decide to go with him?"

"I won't stop you," Ellis steps closer, "but you don't have to make that choice right now."

Ellis picks a handful of blue off the ground and shapes it into a ball, tossing it to Billy. Billy then throws it to Laura. She catches it and chucks it to Ellis. He lifts his feet one at a time and rubs some color from the ball along the soles of his shoes and throws it to Billy once more. With his blue-stained feet, Ellis mimics an ice skater, and slides across the blackened floor leaving color in his wake. Then, he crinkles the surface with his hands to create blades of grass. From the grass he pulls iridescent flowers to make a fantastical looking garden. On the run, toward the grass, Billy throws the ball to Laura. She snatches it from the air with one hand and joins him in the field.

Ellis sets a B.B. King record down on the player and takes a seat under what is left of his wilting apple tree. Bullet squats down by his side and places his head in Ellis's lap. The two of them watch Laura and Billy play catch. Ellis steals a few more glances of their joy, then picks up *The Spy Who Came in from the Cold* and starts reading.

Haunted House

Winter 2031

*E*arly in the morning, birds awaken Hollow Hills with their chattering. The sun struts across the street as Laura approaches her house. A police car is parked in the driveway beside Frank's truck.

Peeking through the front window, Laura can see Frank sitting on the couch, his head in his palms. In front of him sits a female deputy, thirties, her dark hair tucked under her hat, questioning him. The second deputy, a black male in his early forties, stands over the two of them, broad chested with a gun hung along his belt, and a piece of paper in his hand. Laura enters, the sound of the front door absorbs their attention like metal to a magnet.

Frank leaps to his feet, his face red and puffy, and makes a mad dash to wrap her in his arms. His breath steadies in the embrace. Laura's arms slowly raise to hug Frank back. Once around him, she commits and pulls him closer, barely a speck of light able to pass between the tightness of their bodies.

The female deputy interrupts the moment. "Mrs. Nagan, we have a few questions for you."

Frank lets Laura go so she can address the deputy.

"I'm sure you do," Laura reads the deputy's name tag, "Deputy Parsons, and I apologize you even need to be here."

"Where were you, if you don't mind me asking, Mrs. Nagan?" Deputy Parsons continues.

Laura eyes the note in the other deputy's hand, then to his name tag: *Deputy Mattison.*

She exhales. "I'm sure my husband filled you in. It's been rough, to say the least. I set off to do what that letter says, but I couldn't. I decided to go for a long walk instead and ended up having a few drinks at Rebels. Quite a lot of drinks," she says, a light, inappropriate chuckle escaping her lips.

She takes a beat to smoothen out the lies before they leave her mouth. "Ran into an old friend. We bullshitted for a bit. Then, I stumbled off at last call and spent the rest of the night at the playground. Pretty pathetic stuff, officers."

The deputies trade a few more formalities back and forth, before ultimately accepting her explanation. "Alright, Mrs. Nagan. What's important here is that you are safe and I, for one, am happy you decided to stick around," Deputy Parsons tells her.

Laura exhibits a smile of gratitude as the police head for the door. Deputy Mattison hands her a card. Before she can look at it, he says, "Grief counseling. At the community center. They offer group therapy. The card has their number if you need it."

She thanks him and closes the door. Frank paces in the living room. Laura takes a moment to prepare herself for the conversation ahead. Then, enters the living room and sits on the couch. "Let it out, Frank."

He stops his nervous pacing and faces her. "We need to find

a way to communicate again, Laura. I know some things are too far gone, but that note." He joins her on the couch and looks in her eyes. "I don't want to lose you, too. My anger, it made it easy to ignore how you were feeling. I'm sorry for it all. You needed support and I drifted so far away. I resented you."

Laura interrupts. "Frank, I'd hate me, too. I know that because I already hate myself. With a deep, ferocious, and ugly confidence, I fucking HATE me."

Frank takes Laura's hands in his. "Don't say that. It was an accident. A blip in time we can't reverse. But you and I, we can get through this, if we choose to. Walking around like zombies...forfeiting the love we share...it's not the answer." Frank moves closer to Laura. "I miss us. I miss you." He leans in to kiss her. She turns away and stands.

"I am so sorry for leaving you with that note and making you worry. I am. I know your heart is broken and I never wanted to be the one to break it. That beautiful, big heart." She chokes up. "We can't fix this, Frank. I can't give you what you want, and it kills me. This is who I am now. I died that day, too. This-," she motions to herself, "-body in front of you...is just a haunted house."

The statement leaves him speechless. Laura heads upstairs. Frank sits alone. The day sneaks through the blinds, highlighting the defeat on his face.

Dinner for Two

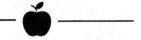

Fall 2030

*I*n the Nagan dining room, Laura sets the table for two. Maroon placemats make for a great marriage with the table's deep, cedar finish. A small basket of apples and oranges lay in the middle of the table, accompanied by a bottle of red wine. The lights are dimmed. The art pieces on the walls have deep pockets of black where the shadows of the room take hold.

Laura returns to the kitchen to peek in the oven where a chicken roasts, while on the stove, vegetable sauté percolates. The refrigerator screen streams a true crime docu-series. Laura stops intermittently to watch a few minutes at a time as she finishes cooking and carrying utensils to the dining room.

The entrance from the garage into the house creaks its way open and fresh air conquers the room. "I told you we need to oil the doors," Laura says loudly. She can hear footsteps approaching.

Frank enters the kitchen, dirty from work, with his work bag over one shoulder. He pulls the cap off his head and runs his fingers through his hair. He walks behind Laura, his eyes fixated on the chicken she pulls from the oven. "Smells good. Where's the tiny human?" he asks, giving Laura a kiss.

"Play date with Steiner turned into a sleepover," Laura explains, "I'm glad he has a friend." Her hands continue to focus on the dinner.

"Good thing for us. Surprise date night." Frank kisses the nape of her neck. The TV catches his attention, the narrator's voice filling his ears. "Ah, I thought you were going to wait for me," he moans. Laura grins at him. "Did the uncle lie about knowing the kid with the, uh, bloody shirt hidden in the barrel?"

Laura opens her mouth to answer.

"Wait, don't tell me. I'll catch up to you," Frank says. He nabs a roasted potato from a pan in front of Laura, to her dismay. "Just going to wash up real quick and be right back down to dig in."

***

The two of them eat dinner over a glass of wine. A smooth evening playlist pumps from a pair of sleek, round speakers hovering inches above a polarity bar on top of a narrow, decorative chest against a wall in the dining room.

Frank finishes up a work story while shoveling the last bit of Brussels sprouts into his mouth. "The damn thing just started spraying mulch everywhere. Hollis, being Hollis, didn't keep his cool. Starts cracking jokes. I'm gritting my teeth. It's like, c'mon man, this is a new client. Button. it. up."

Laura finishes her wine and pours some more.

"But, enough about mulch. Enough about me. What did you get up to without Billy around? Do any painting?"

"No. Just relaxed. Laundry." Laura points at her plate, "Looked up this recipe to see if I could outdo your dinners for once."

Frank lets out a chuckle and takes a sip of wine. "Figured

maybe with the free time you'd dust off the studio." He searches for answers on her face. Laura lowers her gaze to her plate and slices some of her chicken, the smile on her face slowly retracting.

"You know, I was thinking one of these weekends we do a city trip," Frank says.

"The weekends are so busy, Frank." Laura lets out a deep breath. "Between karate and birthday parties and your work hours. I don't know. We don't have time for trips."

"I just, ya know, thought maybe we could visit the galleries. Take Bill to the aerospace museum. He'd love it there."

"Why do you always do this, Frank?"

"Do what?"

"You get so fixated on wanting me to paint or see paintings or buy paint. It's just, why?"

Frank drops his utensils into the plate. "What do you want me to say, Laura? That I feel bad that you don't do a thing you loved doing?"

"You don't feel bad, Frank. You feel guilty. For something you shouldn't feel guilty about. I just wanted to have a nice dinner and for once not go down this road," Laura retorts.

"So, I'm the bad guy for taking you away from it and also the bad guy for wanting to bring you back to it?"

Laura scoffs and stands up with her plate in her hand, pushing her chair out of the way. "You don't listen anymore. You didn't take me away from anything. I chose this life with you because it's what I wanted." She enters the kitchen to wash her plate, leaving Frank alone at the table.

Frank exhales, then purses his lips, the music his only company. He stirs the last bit of wine in his glass and swallows it. "Music, off," he says. The music stops playing. He gathers his dirty plate along with the empty glass and walks into the kitchen.

Laura is loading the dishwasher with what she's just rinsed off.

Frank joins her at the sink and turns on the faucet to scrub his plate of scraps. Laura holds out her hand for the plate. Frank passes it to her. She puts it in the dishwasher. Then, he runs the garbage disposal for a few seconds and turns it back off once all the food clears it.

He rips a paper towel from a roll on the counter in front of them and dries his hands. "I'm sorry, Laura. I worry so much that I'm going to mess this whole family thing up that the worrying ends up being the exact fucking thing to mess it up. I'm sorry I can't get out of my own way."

She places her hand atop his, which rests on the edge of the sink. "I'll forgive you IF...you tell me my Brussels sprouts are better than yours," she bargains with a smirk.

"Hmmm," Frank thinks to himself, then toys with Laura, "a little undercooked if you ask me."

Laura hits him with a potholder. "You fucker!" The room fills with their laughter.

No Time for Fear

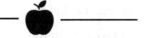

Spring 1948

A storm rages. The rain pelts against the roof of the Foster household and gusts of wind howl like a pack of hungry wolves. Ellis watches over the back of the couch, through a window, as lightning cuts through the pitch-black sky, bringing with it the mighty roar of thunder. All throughout the house lights flicker.

Headlights fill Ellis's peripheral. Then, they turn off. Moments later the front door busts open, bringing along the rain. Ellis jumps off the couch and stares at the door. His father, drenched, tosses his work bag on the floor. He slams the door shut behind him, removes his wet jacket and hangs it up.

"No fire?" Michael says, disappointed at the empty fireplace. The lights continue to flicker. "Get the candles," he barks.

Ellis makes a mad dash to a kitchen pantry and gathers as many candles as he can into his arms. He runs back to the living room, where his father has begun piling whatever dry wood left into the fireplace. The lights cut out and Ellis trips, dropping the candles across the living room floor. "God dammit, boy," his father grumbles.

Ellis gets to his knees to pick up the candles. Michael removes a zippo from his back pocket and lights it, guiding himself to one of the candles on the floor. He lights the candle and places it on the coffee table. Ellis picks up a few more and hands them to his father, who lights them and scatters them about the house. One, he carries to the fireplace so he can finish building the fire he started. He stuffs kindling in between the logs and gets it ablaze quickly.

The rain beats heavier than before. Thunder claps as if it were in the room with them. Intermittently, the entire house comes alive from encroaching flashes of lightning. Ellis, paralyzed in his shoes, shudders at the loud cracks of thunder.

"No time for fear," his father shouts at him.

The screen door at the back of the kitchen bangs repeatedly against the house. Michael heads through the kitchen, opens the backdoor, and locks the screen door with a latch. Ellis watches his father from behind, the candlelight flickering with the rain.

A bolt of lightning careens from the sky and strikes the tree in their backyard, ripping a hole in its trunk. Michael jumps back and trips, causing Ellis to nearly leap out of his shoes. The hole in the tree emits smoke. A collection of branches break and drop from residual damage taken during the strike. Smoke continues to pour from where the lightning landed. A small flame eventually crawls from the hole, fighting for its life with the rain.

Ellis approaches and stands beside his father, his tiny body almost invisible, as the two of them watch the tree burn from within itself. They watch for nearly an hour as fire finds new holes to exit. Eventually, the flames are no match for the rain. They subside along with the smoke.

Michael closes the backdoor and shrugs over to the refrigerator.

He opens it hastily and gets himself a beer. He slumps on the couch to relax. A partially smoked cigar sits in an ashtray on the coffee table. He picks it up, lights it with a candle, and takes a few puffs. Ellis stands in the doorway between the living room and kitchen, watching his father alternate between smoking and drinking. Michael feels Ellis's eyes on him.

"Bed. Now," he orders.

***

Later that evening, Michael, still sitting on the couch, nods off with a line of beer cans in front of him on the coffee table. The cigar in his mouth falls out and lands on his chest. The heat builds through his t-shirt until the burn jolts him awake. He sends the cigar flying with his hand. It rolls across the floor and stops before the fireplace, where the fire is dying out.

He gets himself to his feet and stumbles around the coffee table. He bends down to pick up the cigar and tosses it into the fireplace. Pausing before the fire, he glares at the flames, watching the wood burn into ash. His tired eyes reflect the flickers of the fire. When he turns back, he steps into melting wax from one of the candles Ellis had dropped earlier. In his drunken state, he loses equilibrium and falls backwards into the mantle place, knocking the urn onto the ground. The top pops off and the ashes spill as it rolls sideways across the floor. In a panic, Michael drops to his knees and retrieves it. He flails, scooping the remains back into it, but most have coagulated from touching the moistened floorboards. "No, no, no, please," he cries out, collecting handfuls of ash. He soon realizes it's useless and gives up. Sitting in the mess, he turns his soot-covered palms toward himself and weeps into his hands.

Ellis hears the commotion and creeps down the staircase, frozen at the sight of his father on his knees, crying. Slowly, he retreats and one bellowing creak from the stairs gives him up. His father lowers his hands and spots him on the steps.

Michael climbs to his feet yelling, "You! You're the reason she's gone! You little bastard!" The drunk lunges into the kitchen, grabs one of the chairs at the table and flings it at the staircase without a second thought. Ellis cowers as it hits the rails in front of him. He then runs back up into his room, slamming the door behind himself. Below, his father continues shouting incoherently. Ellis covers his ears with his hands, rocking back and forth on his bed.

***

Ellis remains in his bedroom the following morning and into the afternoon. Occasionally, he reaches for the doorknob but immediately retracts when he hears movement downstairs. The noise eventually subsides, and he exits into the upstairs hallway. His father's door is closed. With caution, he walks downstairs. The chair is back at the kitchen table. Through the backdoor he sees his father dragging something across the yard to where the tree used to stand.

Ellis steps outside. You wouldn't even know a storm came through the night before, as the sun shines hot from a clear blue sky. The ravaged tree is now uprooted in pieces across the lawn. A crater in the earth sits where it once was. At the edge of the hole is the urn. Next to that, his father cuts burlap from a brand-new sapling. Michael's hands are wrapped in bloody rags that match fresh red stains on the handle of a shovel by his feet. With the infant tree completely uncovered, Michael picks up the urn. He mouths a few words Ellis can't hear and places the urn into the hole. Without turning to acknowledge the boy's presence Michael says, "Grab the other shovel."

Ellis walks to the shed, grabs a shovel, and joins his father at the hole. The urn sits dead center in the dirt. His father picks up his shovel, scoops some loose dirt from a mound he created digging the hole, and tosses it over the urn. Ellis does the same. They trade back and forth until the metal canister is no longer visible. Michael places the new tree in the hole. Ellis helps his father fill in around the small tree. It takes most of the rest of the day. Michael flattens the last shovelful of dirt. The two of them wipe the sweat from their heads.

Michael goes into the house and remerges a few minutes later with a beer and glass of lemonade. He hands the lemonade to Ellis and cracks the beer for himself. They both take a refreshing gulp of their beverage and admire the tree they've planted.

"How big will it get?" Ellis asks.

His father swallows another sip of beer.

"Only time will tell, son."

You're a Saint

Winter 2031

*F*rank sits at his desk at work, trying to concentrate, with little luck. Deep, dark rings inhabit the bags living beneath his eyes. His office is sizable, with reddish-brown walls and huge windows that face a small parking lot. A few spaces are filled with ultramodern vans and trucks that have "Nagan Lawn & Land" decaled on their sides, accompanied by the logo of three bright, bushy trees.

A bookshelf, containing company records and legal documents, occupies one corner of the office. Beside it is a cozy, blue couch that pops among the decor. The wall opposite the door is covered with a hand-painted mural of the company name and logo. On the wall to his left hangs an abstract painting of what appears to be three shadowy figures in a sea of differing colors. The lower right corner has the initials *L.H.* painted on it. Frank leans back in his leather chair and stares at it. Regret contorts his face and the weight of it settles in his eyes.

In his silence, Frank turns back to his desk, only to be assaulted by a litany of photos of the family he used to have. One draws him in. It's a candid shot of Laura pushing Billy on a swing in autumn. Frank's eyes trade regret for grief. He can't take it and turns the frame picture side down atop the desk. A knock on the door breaks his train of thought. "Come in."

The doorknob twists and a young woman emerges, her suit tightly fit against her petite body. Her blonde hair is tied up in a messy bun and the floor echoes under her shoes. She uses a stylus to shuffle through appointments on a tablet she carries, while a small cylindrical earpiece sits perfectly in her ear.

"Maisy," Frank says, "What's on the docket?"

"Hold one second, sir," Maisy says, as she taps the earpiece.

"Sir, Brian Billips is on the phone complaining about how our guys backed into his new sign. You also have a call with the high school about contract renewal at one."

"Tell Brian I'll be right over."

***

At the store, Mr. Billips is already outside, smoking a cigarette while Frank's workers stand alongside him. He's an overweight, balding man, with big rim glasses and a bushy mustache. Frank parks by his company's truck and walks over to the group.

"How about you guys work around the perimeter?" Frank suggests, fastening his pace towards Mr. Billips.

"How goes it, Frank?" Brian's deep voice cuts through the air and reaches Frank.

"Brian," says Frank, ignoring the question, "Apologies about this mishap."

The two shake hands and walk towards the sign.

Brian instinctually asks, "How's the family?"

Both men tense up and Brian recoils. "Sorry, Frank. Honest mistake. No offense."

"None taken. It's an adjustment for everyone," Frank says, bending down to examine the sign. "Oh, they really rocked this baby, huh?"

"It could've been worse, but it's a brand-new sign, Frank."

"I'll have it fixed up by tomorrow. Don't worry. I'll cover any repairs or replacements needed on what I don't have the material to fix it with myself. How about that?"

"Thank ya, Frank."

Frank stands and looks across the parking lot to his men pulling tools off the truck. His eyes then follow them to a fallen tree on the property. "In the meantime, I'll help these guys get that tree cleaned up for you, so we are out of your hair as soon as possible."

"You're a saint, Frank." Brian smiles, putting his cigarette out in a wet napkin he removes from his pocket. The men shake hands once more and Brian returns to the store.

Frank and his workers spend the afternoon clearing the tree from Mr. Billips's property. The workers chatter constantly about a lot of nothing, while Frank hardly utters a word over the rip of his chainsaw. After the tree is cleared, Frank heads into the SuperMart to pick up a few things. Bread, deli meats, butter, pancake mix, and syrup fill his basket. He turns a corner toward the cash register and pauses before a display of juice boxes. He pulls a six-pack of grape Hi-C from the stack and holds it out before him. A lump hardens in his throat. He chokes back the emotion frothing in his eyes and puts the pack back on the shelf, continuing to the register where a redheaded woman in her sixties waits to ring him up.

"Hiya, Frank. Haven't seen you in some time. My thoughts and prayers are with you and Laura. Every single night, I pray," the cashier says.

"Thank you, Leigh," Frank says.

The two don't say much more than that. With a small scanner wrapped around the end of her finger, Leigh scans the items with a tap on the barcode and proceeds to bag them in a reusable bag Frank hands her. He removes his phone from his pocket and waves it over the credit card machine. The machine accesses his account and approves the sale. Leigh and he exchange farewell pleasantries and he leaves.

The Uninvited Guest

Winter 2031

*O*n the way home, Frank passes by the stop-and-ride along the cliffs of Western Pass. He notices Laura's car is parked in the lot and comes to a stop. He pulls in and parks beside her, using his phone to call her. No answer. He tries again. Nothing.

He gets out and examines the small lot. He's alone. He looks through the windows of her car for any clues. Nothing seems out of place. He walks to the edge of the stop-and-ride, hops the guardrail and glances over the cliff, down into the calm water below. "Laura!"

He is met with silence.

Louder and more frantic. "Laura!"

He makes his way across the street to enter the woods. A few feet past the tree line he calls for her. Then, he uses his phone. She doesn't answer. He alternates between shouting her name and calling her number as he moves deeper into the woods. Erratic in his steps, he loses track of where he is and can no longer see the parking lot from where he stands. The bare bones of the trees and a chilling quiet buried into the cold air are all that surround him.

He takes a deep breath to collect himself and stops pacing. He pulls his phone back out and dials 9-1-1 but before he can hit send, he hears movement and voices nearby. He bends down and picks up a log to protect himself. At the end of the voices emerges Laura, with Ellis by her side, much to his surprise and him to theirs.

"Laura," he says. His face coupled with relief and confusion.

Laura stops frozen in her tracks.

"What's going on, Laura?" Frank's eyes shift from her to Ellis. "Where were you? And who is this?"

She is at a loss and looks to Ellis.

"We should show him. It's the right thing to do," Ellis suggests.

She hesitates and volunteers no words.

Frank contains confrontation. "Show me what?"

"Come with me, Frank," Laura says.

The three of them venture through the woods, Frank throwing questions along the way, wanting to know where they are going, who Ellis is, and why they were out there together.

"You wouldn't believe me if I told you. It's best if you see it," Laura tells him.

He hushes but remains defensive. They finally reach the tree. Ellis places his hand over the carving in the bark and opens the gateway.

Frank can't believe his eyes. "What the fuck?"

"Welcome to JoJo. She's safe," Ellis says, waving Frank in.

"Says some strange guy who's out here with my wife," Frank remarks to Ellis.

"Come with me, Frank. Please," Laura says.

***

With trepidation, Frank steps through the opening and into the void, struck with wonder at the remarkable landscapes. "What is this place?"

Ellis creates a swirl with his pointer finger in a patch of red grass.

"Some kind of magic," Laura says.

Frank is having a hard time splitting his attention between Laura and the otherworldly beauty of the place. Laura takes his hand, whispering, "Come."

They walk into the red field. She touches his palm to a purple sunflower, a bit of the plum tone rubbing off on his hand. "Go ahead," Laura tells him.

He makes a purple circle against the yellow sky above them. She puts her finger in the circle and drags some of the purple across the sky to make a cloud. She can feel his eyes on her and turns to meet them. Frank stutters for words, but instead opts for a soft, warm smile.

Laura breaks the silence. "There's more, Frank."

A tiny hand grabs his, pressing its soft skin against his rough hand. He retracts his gaze from Laura and looks down. It's Billy. His skin is alive with a throbbing pulse of green and yellow. Frank drops the boy's hand to cover his mouth, frozen through and bordering shock. In a disconcerting whisper, Frank utters, "Billy?"

Billy wraps his arms against Frank's waist. Frank, still stunned, eases his way back to his son and kneels. He warms up to the surreal moment and wraps his arms around Billy. He unlocks the hug and kisses the boy on the head. Then, grabs him by the cheeks with both hands to look into his eyes. And, like how the deer speaks to Ellis, Billy speaks to Frank, subliminally, rendering the grieving father to a sopping, wet mess. "Hi, daddy. I love you. I've missed you."

A rainbow forms around Frank's knees like an oil slick in the rain. The puddle runs along the ground to the apple tree, contacting its trunk. Frank looks up to the green sky changing and mixing with colors. His eyes pause at both Laura and Ellis, astonished. "How?"

Before either can answer, another figure steps forward from

the apple tree. An older man, with a similar visage to Frank, but more worn and weathered in the face. He commands all their attention. Frank stands up and squints the familiar figure into focus.

Laura stands closest to the figure. She recognizes it. "Holy shit, Frankie Sr.?"

The man is mostly colorless, except for some dull grays and colder tones of black and blue. He plucks an apple from the tree he's stepped from and it turns black in his hand. He moves like a bruise through the void, stopping to look into Laura's eyes. His gaze is cold and cruel. Laura backs away from him, wrapping her arms around herself. Billy, frightened, runs towards Laura and hides, peeping out from behind her.

Frank Sr. steps closer to Frank, a hateful glare laser focused on his son. Parts of the elder are completely transparent like an unfinished image in a coloring book. His shadow morphs into a tentacled beast behind him that flails along the surroundings.

Ellis watches from the red field, attentive and ready for anything.

Frank Sr. is now toe-to-toe with Frank Jr., who is nearly hyperventilating. "Pop...," Frank gasps, breathless. His attention shifts to the shadowed tentacles. "Once a monster, always a monster."

Sr. extends his colorless hand and grabs Frank's shoulder, sending a shock through the younger man's body, locking him in a seizure. He, then, uses his other hand to shove the blackened apple into Frank Jr.'s mouth, trying to force it down his throat. The ground under Frank Jr.'s feet decays as his body writhes in his father's powerful grip. The red grass turns gray and black. The purple clouds evaporate. The abstract peace siphons away with the vibrant colors and a never-before-seen rot spiderwebs throughout the void, shrouding everything it touches in a shadow of darkness.

The bleak poison slimes its way against Billy's foot and the boy begins to melt. "Mom!" Billy cries telepathically. Laura panics and, with little success, attempts to scoop up the parts of him dissolving. Ellis runs to her, picks up what remains of Billy, and hurries him to the apple tree. His little body binds back into the mysterious place beyond the void.

Ellis sprints to Frank, who is still locked in a trance at the end of his father's fingers. He grabs onto Sr.'s arm and is taken by the same darkness, unable to break the abnormality's grip. The erosion continues to spread. The luminosity is vacuumed away from every spot it brushes against. Out of total desperation and absolute confusion, Laura goes to her husband and whispers in his ear, "I love you, Frank. Please, stay."

Sr. shrieks as Frank coughs up the rotten apple. Laura turns his head and kisses him. Her lips work. They free Frank from the clutches of his father. Laura releases Frank's mouth from hers and he falls to the ground. Sr. swipes downward but before he's able to contact Frank, he turns to dust.

"You're okay, Frank," Laura reassures him.

Frank retracts from Laura and gets to his feet, exiting in a hurry.

"Frank!" Laura yells, but he is already gone.

Ellis chases after him, followed by Laura.

"Frank, stop. Slow down," Ellis hollers.

It only makes Frank run faster. He continues through the woods, never looking back. Out of breath, he falls to his knees in front of his truck, trying to steal any air his lungs can get. Laura and Ellis catch up. She kneels next to him, stroking his back gently to help him breathe.

"Why'd you bring me here?" he snaps, scaring Laura away.

"Fra-"

"Laura, that is not real, none of it is real. That thing isn't our son. We need to stay away."

"Billy wa...,"

"Billy is dead, Laura. He's dead!" The words are an arrow through her heart. "And you-" Frank says, pointing at Ellis, "Stay away from me and my wife."

Ellis remains quiet.

Laura approaches Frank, again.

"We should go home, Frank, where we can talk about what happened." Laura helps him up and steers him toward his car. "I'll follow right behind you, okay?"

She turns back. Ellis is gone.

Returns

Winter 1983

*E*llis sits, leaning against the withered apple tree. Bullet cozies up by his side, licking the fur along one of his front legs. Both are surrounded by black pockets spotted along landscapes of faded grays. Bullet stops cleaning himself and shifts his attention toward the entrance of the void. It opens as it did in 1967. Ellis gets to his feet and walks to the opening. He sticks his hand through to make sure it's real. Then, kneels to face Bullet.

"I won't be back, my friend."

Downtown is once again similar but different. The cars that line the streets are sportier, with pointed fronts and flashy bodies. Most of the younger people Ellis passes wear clothing with zigzag designs and bold colors. One girl keeps her hair up and tight in a neon scrunchy. Her mother walks behind her with a big blowout, wearing a thick-shouldered coat. Men bundle up in loads of denim, their jackets often matching their jeans.

Ellis stares into a store, MovieRama. Customers are looking through shelves of tapes in boxes with movie posters on them. Above the cashier, in the back, a square television hangs from the ceiling, playing a movie. The intense scene is of mother and son trapped in their car, while a dog attacks from outside. It consumes Ellis and he enters, walking up to the counter to speak with the clerk. "What is this place?"

"MovieRama, Hollow Hills one-stop-shop for all the latest movie rentals. Can I help you find something?" The jovial employee responds. "This is *Cujo*. I highly recommend it. Great Stephen King adaptation, if you ask me."

"Who is Stephen King?" Ellis asks, stunning the video clerk.

"Only the greatest author in modern times," the over enthusiastic man tells Ellis. "Want to rent it?"

"No, I think I'd rather read the book," Ellis answers, reading the clerk's name tag, "Thanks though, Martin."

Ellis investigates a few of the movies on the shelves, reading their plots and admiring the cover art on the boxes. A few people mill around him making their choices. He watches a bit more of *Cujo* as another employee, older than the clerk, passes him in the direction of the door. The older associate struggles to open a drawer in the wall to the side of the entrance. It finally budges and a few tapes fall out onto the floor.

"Martin, you wanna keep working here, you better start doing your job. This isn't a free movie theater," the man yells at the clerk.

Martin sprints to the front of the store, "Sorry, Mr. Linton. I'm on it." He haphazardly picks the tapes up off the floor and begins digging more from the drop box while his boss watches over him.

"The returns need to be checked back in at the beginning of every shift. If I gotta warn ya one more time, that's it," Mr. Linton says, before walking away.

Another employee comes to assist Martin. She takes a few tapes from his arms and says, "He's a dick. Don't let him get to you, Moo."

The sound of the nickname gives Ellis pause. He stares at the two employees much too long. They notice. "Can we help you, sir?" asks Moo.

Ellis shakes his head and exits the store.

He continues down main street, past the busiest parts and up into streets occupied by houses. Standing outside his childhood home, he notices the fresh blue paint covering it. He spends a few minutes staring at the tree in the backyard. All its leaves have fallen, exposing the barren brown trunk. The ends of its branches fluttered in the wind. It looked smaller somehow.

A younger woman opens the front door. "Can I help you?" she asks the disheveled looking Ellis.

He waves to her and says, "No, I was admiring your tree. Beautiful even without the leaves."

The woman's face contorts at the odd statement. "I guess."

Ellis waves goodbye and walks away. He trudges through the cold another four blocks or so west, eventually ending up in front of Marie's house. It's been painted red. The front yard is flat and bare. The porch has a wooden bench on it in place of her rocking chair, and the fence surrounding the property has been modernized.

Ellis walks up the empty driveway and hops a locked gate to gain access to the side of the house. He peeks through a first-floor window. The lights are off inside. He creeps low around the house onto the back porch. At the backdoor, he crouches and starts rustling exposed bricks in the foundation of the house. The first few don't budge, and then finally one comes loose. Ellis removes it and sticks his hand in the hole. Out comes a mason jar full of money. He sticks it in his sweater pocket.

A Night's Rest

Winter 1983

*E*llis sits alone in a booth at the Roundabout Diner. A waitress, close to his age, approaches. He nervously says, "A burger and some fries."

"What about a drink?

He reads her name tag. "Umm, a milkshake, Cassandra."

She jots down his order onto a pad and heads to the kitchen.

The diner is fairly empty. An older couple shares a meal a couple of booths away. A middle-aged man sips some coffee from a stool at a counter that runs the length of the room. A sign that reads *Janitor Wanted* is taped at the end of the counter.

The waitress returns with a tray full of food and slides it to him. "Here's your food, hon! And your bill. No rush."

"Do you still need a janitor?" Ellis asks.

Cassandra looks back at the sign. "Oh that, you need to talk to

Del, the manager. He's the little, angry guy at the cash register. See him when you pay."

Ellis acquiesces and shifts his attention to the food. He says Grace the way Marie taught him. Then, he scarfs up the burger and washes it down with his milkshake.

At the cash counter, Ellis asks the manager about the janitor position. Del gives Ellis a once over. "Can you clean yourself up a bit and start tomorrow?"

"Yes," Ellis says, enthusiastically.

***

Close to sundown, Ellis enters Rebels with a brown shopping bag. He orders a Coca-Cola from the bartender and heads to the bathroom, where he empties the contents of the bag into a sink. A bar of soap, deodorant, a toothbrush, and toothpaste. With the toothbrush, he scrubs at his teeth with force, scraping it along his tongue, and spitting the mouthful of toothpaste into the sink. Lastly, he removes his shirt and washes his upper body with soap and water, drying himself with paper towels and applying deodorant.

Back at the bar, Ellis keeps to himself, babysitting his soda. The brown bag of toiletries sits in his lap. A television behind the bar plays MTV. Ellis taps his feet along to the music videos. The bartender occasionally asks if he needs anything as the hours pass. "Another coke," is his only reply.

The clock strikes 2:00 AM and the lights come on. Ellis hesitates until the bartender eyes him to leave. He finishes his drink, buttons up his sweater and exits into the bitter cold, where a couple of drunks smoke cigarettes and chatter loudly. Ellis stands away from them by the door, clutching the shopping bag, wrapping his arms around himself to stay warm. A short, bald man with a gravelly voice holds out his cigarette to Ellis. "It'll keep you warm," the man says.

"No, thank you," Ellis says.

The other two men finish their cigarettes and head off into the

106

night, leaving Ellis alone with the man who offered him a smoke. "The name's Clay. Never seen ya eer before. New to town?"

"Feels like it. I grew up here. Haven't been back for a long time."

Clay exhales a cloud of smoke. "Why the fuck would ya ever come back to Hollow Hills?"

"I don't plan on staying long. Looking to make enough money to move."

"Gotta get a job first," Clay jokes. His chuckle echoes in the lonely air.

"I start at the Roundabout tomorrow."

Clay thinks a moment, sizing Ellis up, then says, "You got nowhere to go, huh? Back in town. Soda pops at a bar. Cleaned yourself up in the bathroom. Stayed until the lights scared all us roaches away... ya ain't got a place to stay."

Clay takes another drag, his gaze still on Ellis.

Ellis looks down to his feet, avoiding the truth.

"Kid, a lot of us ain't got no place to stay. No judgment from me. Shit, I'm about to head to the shelter. You're more than welcome to tag along...guy-who-still-ain't-told-me-his-name." Clay throws his cigarette to the ground and rubs it out under his ratty sneakers, immediately lighting another.

"Ellis. My name is Ellis."

The two of them walk south, down toward the docks. Clay stuffs one hand in his pocket, walking lazily with his cigarette in the other, controlling most of the conversation. "I was a star footballer in high school, but injured myself before college, ya know? This place sucked my soul away after. Dreams crushed. No future. I became trapped here in Hollow fucking Hills. Always hated that name. We ain't got any hills, just a cliff." Clay's thoughts trail off.

"You don't work?" asks Ellis.

"Eh, I've had a laundry list of jobs over the years. None for too long," he says, wiping snot along his sleeve. "Had my fair share of run-ins with the law. Kinda makes it hard to find a steady gig. Right now, I do deliveries for Mario, the butcher over on Carlson. The cheapskate owes me back-pay."

The two men approach the shelter.

"Do you live here?" Ellis asks.

"Most nights I bunk up at the Wayward. You can pay by the hour, but it's been slower than a snail so this will havta do for tonight."

They enter the small gymnasium. A nun greets and directs them to two neighboring cots with fresh sheets, a pillow, and wool blanket. They sit on their respective beds.

"Could be worse," Clay says. He takes his jacket and shoes off, settling in.

Ellis follows suit and stares quietly at the ceiling while others snore, scratch, and mumble around him.

Come morning, Ellis wakes to find Clay's cot empty.

A man's voice emerges. "Your friend, he's in the mess hall."

Ellis turns to locate who's speaking to him. The man is lean, his shabby clothes torn in multiple places, and skin covered with red spots.

"Breakfast is in the cafeteria connected to the gym," the man says, "Better get to it before they don't have any left. Whatever you do, don't eat the eggs. You'll get the runs."

Several nuns and regular clothed volunteers work a buffet line, serving those who spent the night and others who have walked in off the street. Clay sits at a corner seat of a full table, eating sloppily, shoving food into his face without using silverware. Ellis joins him.

"Not bad, but not as good as what I ate when I was locked up. Imagine that? Prisoners gettin' fed better than the homeless." Clay laughs, yanking a hunk of pancake with his teeth. Ellis enjoys his food meticulously, cutting every bite deliberately and savoring them as if they were his last.

Clay jaws on until they finish eating and then accompanies Ellis into town to the Roundabout.

"Ask the fella who owns this joint if there are any other openings, will ya?" Clay asks. Ellis exhibits his discomfort at the question.

"Eh, that was too much, I know. It's your first day. I'll leave ya be. You know where to find me later, if you need a friend, Ellie boy," Clay says, before walking off.

Less Than Not Much

Winter 1983

*E*llis enters the diner. Several people are seated throughout the booths, happily chatting alongside mild jazz playing low from overhead speakers. "Elvin," Del shouts, as he comes through the swinging kitchen doors, "Hit the storage closet. Overalls, mop, bucket. Everything you need to start cleaning is in there."

"Everything looks clean," Ellis wonders aloud.

"It is, because I keep a spotless front room. You need to hit the head. One of these animals clogged the toilet," Del says, leaving Ellis with his thoughts.

Ellis changes into overalls and gets right to work plunging the toilet. Then, he changes a few dim bulbs over the booths, sweeps in the lulls between patrons, and empties the trash into a dumpster out back. The waitress, Cassandra, who served him the day before, sits outside on her break, smoking a cigarette. She offers the butt to Ellis.

He respectfully turns her down.

"Ellis, right?"

He nods in agreement.

"Guessing you're new in town?"

"I grew up here, but haven't been back in years," he tells her, shy in both body language and delivery.

Cassandra stands up and approaches him to study his face. The smell of her cigarette hovers around her. "Hmm, I can't say I recognize you and we couldn't have been that far apart in school."

Ellis takes a step back. "I was homeschooled. Moved away when I was ten. I don't plan on staying too long this time either."

"That makes two of us. I tell myself that every single day," Cassandra says, a shred of disappointment she's still there.

The backdoor opens and Del sticks his head out. "This isn't a social club. Back to work, both of you."

Ellis hurries back inside. Cassandra casually puts her cigarette out against the side of the dumpster and tosses it over the open top.

As the sun lowers in the sky, Ellis cleans the front windows and puts down salt on the sidewalk, casually watching people come and go. Del steps outside for a smoke break. He holds out the pack to Ellis, who declines. "You did good today, Ellis," Del says, lighting the cigarette, "I like a man that minds their own and does the work. These kids nowadays. They're lazy and unprofessional. Crazy clothes and hair. They could learn a thing from you."

Ellis sprinkles another cup of salt on the ground as he listens.

Del checks his watch. "You can call it a day, kid. Same time tomorrow. Maybe some evenings on the weekends."

"That's fine with me. Whatever you need," Ellis says.

"So, you always lived in Hollow Hills?" Del asks.

"When I was real young. Moved away for a bit and just got back into town."

"Got family here, still?"

"Not anymore."

"So, where you staying?"

"The shelter down by the waterfront."

"No, that won't do," Del says, removing the cigarette from his mouth. He puts it out against the sidewalk and opens the diner door to stick his head in. "Cassandra, hold down the fort. I'll be back soon."

Del walks Ellis a few blocks away to a two-story building that's in need of a new paint job and some major exterior renovation. Inside, the two of them pass a woman exiting a downstairs apartment.

"The first is right around the corner, Mags," Del says to her as she passes.

"Yeah, yeah, you pain in the ass," she replies. Del smirks.

"Got a room for you upstairs," he tells Ellis, leading him to the staircase.

The second-floor hallway is dank and smells of mildew. Del fumbles with a key ring and unlocks the first door to the right. He turns on the light and invites Ellis in. It's a tiny room, with a single bed, mid-size dresser, small refrigerator, and a hot plate. Del opens the blinds at the only window in the room. "Listen, I know it's not much. It's honestly less than not much, but I can't have you down at the shelter. That wouldn't sit well with me."

"I love it," Ellis says.

"That's a first," Del says, while he grabs some sheets from the closet and throws them on the bed, "You got hot water, heat, gas for the stove, and electricity. The deal is seventy-five a week. I'll take it straight from your pay. Sound good?"

"Yeah, sounds good. Thanks."

Del removes the key from the keyring and puts it in Ellis's hand. "Good. I'll let you make yourself at home. See you tomorrow, Ellis."

Making Friends

———— 🍎 ————

Winter 1983

*E*llis keeps his head down and works the winter away. Most of his free time is spent at the library for books and records. From time to time he shares lunch with Cassandra, never really giving much detail on who he is. Week by week, he saves his money and doesn't bat an eye in the direction of Western Pass.

On his walk home one Friday, he is interrupted by a yell from across the street. "Elroy!"

Clay stands, waving in his direction, wearing a white apron, next to an idling cargo van.

"Clay!" Ellis waves back as he crosses the street. "It's Ellis, by the way," he adds.

"Sorry, pal-o-mine. Yer looking good, Ellis. Haven't seen ya in a bit. Where ya staying?"

Ellis points to the multi-family house across the street.

"Renting a room for now. From my boss."

Clay approves, "Nice. Nice," scratching his bald head, "Ya know, my shift's about to end. Maybe we can hang out or something?"

"I was going to sit in and read," Ellis murmurs.

"Okay, but what if I told you I could make us some steaks, you like steaks, right? Everybody likes steaks," Clay says, speaking like a salesman at a used car lot. "Mario won't miss 'em. That greedy fuck. I always have a coupla extra lying around," Clay continues, removing an ice chest from the side of the van. He opens it to show Ellis the cuts of meat. "C'mon, Ellis. Just a dinner between two friends and I'll be outta yer hair."

Ellis salivates at the sight of the filets and says, "Alright. A dinner among friends."

"Atta boy!" Clay smacks Ellis on the back.

The two of them enjoy the steaks in Ellis's apartment. The top of his dresser is now lined with books from the library. On a small end table near the bed is an old record player spinning George Clinton. Clay sits in front of empty beer bottles, cracking jokes and telling outrageous stories about the women he's slept with and trophies he won in high school. Ellis sips a glass of Cola.

"I feel like I do all the talking. A real motormouth I am," Clay says. He gets up to grab another beer from the refrigerator. "Don't ya got anything to say, a story, questions, anything?"

Ellis sits straight, unsure of what to say.

Clay messes with Ellis's hair, laughing. "We gotta loosen ya up. Sure ya don't want a beer? One ain't gonna kill ya."

Ellis refuses and collects their empty plates. He places them in the sink, then goes to the end table and puts money from his pocket into the mason jar, which is now overflowing with savings.

Clay nearly chokes on his beer. "That's quite the stack ya got there, my friend. Ya just going to keep saving that and not enjoying it?" Ellis twists the jar shut, places it back and closes the drawer. "A real shame," Clay says.

"What do you mean?"

Clay steps closer to Ellis. "I mean, we only got one life, Ellie boy. One measly stinkin' life. Ya really want to carry on never taking a moment of that life to enjoy it? When I first met ya, you had nothing. Now, ya got a job, a place, and savings. That's because of hard work, my man. And ya know what? Sometimes ya gotta celebrate hard work by taking a bit of yer nut and using it to do the celebrating."

"I don't know," Ellis mutters.

Clay wraps his arm around Ellis's shoulder, pulling him close. "Listen, I know. Ya wanna get outta this hell hole. I commend ya for being so dedicated to that idea." He sloppily tries to salute, his breath stinking of beer. "But having one good night isn't the end of the world. So, ya gotta work one more day than ya planned to. No biggie. Do ya really wanna go yer whole life never taking time to have fun and only worrying about surviving? That's no life, my friend. No life at all."

Ellis thinks to himself. He looks around the room. Then, to Clay's drunken smile, hope lingering in his eyes. "Okay, one night," Ellis says.

Clay claps his hands together. "Hot damn! That's what I'm talking about, Ellis."

Wayward Souls

———— 🍎 ————

Winter 1983

*H*ours deep into partying, they occupy a room at the Wayward Motel with two of Clay's friends, Jay, a burly, hairy beast of a man, and Walton, a scraggly, long-haired man with yellow teeth. Empty beer and liquor bottles are scattered about. Some slack on the couch, some on the floor. Ellis is drunk, listening to the men jaw on about work, government conspiracies, and women.

"You're a good-looking guy. You must have some good fuck stories," Walton says to Ellis. "Spill the beans."

"I'm not hungry," Ellis responds, his mind numb from the alcohol.

"Clay, this guy's gone. Not food, my man. Women," Jay says, followed by laughter.

Clay removes a bag of cocaine from his pocket and snorts a line off the coffee table. "Yeah, man, ya probably pull some great tail with a face like that."

Jay and Walton join Clay in railing lines.

Ellis sits up in his seat. "What's that?"

"You never had coke?" Walton asks.

"It's my favorite pop," Ellis says.

All the men burst into laughter. Clay moves closer to Ellis on the couch and chops up another line. He takes a rolled-up dollar from the table and hands it to Ellis. "Try it. You'll meet God," Clay admits.

Ellis looks at the dollar, then the white powder stretched into a thin line on the table. He leans forward and does what he saw the rest of them do. One inhale and it hits him like a freight train. He winces and rubs his watering eyes, sniffling with his nose even harder. "Ride it out, Ellis. Ride it out," Clay tells him, rubbing his back.

"And stop stalling on that pussy story," Jay shouts.

"What's pussy?" Ellis asks, sincerely.

The men collapse laughing. Ellis becomes embarrassed. Clay hushes them up. "Hey. No shame in being a late bloomer. But we gotta rectify this tonight, Ellie boy," he says, tapping Ellis's back. "Jay, go make a call," Clay instructs his friend.

Jay gets up and leaves the motel room. Walton stumbles across the room looking for more beer. Clay indulges in more cocaine. The three of them sit and watch television, waiting for Jay's return. Within the hour, two women, dressed in heavy jackets and high boots enter the room along with Jay.

"Fran, Lil," Walton says. He winks at the women.

They remove their jackets and join the men in partying. The blonde, Fran, wearing a tight yellow dress with long cheetah print boots to go with it, sits in Walton's lap, while the brunette, Lil, in jean shorts and a sheer shirt over a tank top, settles into Jay's. Fran bends forward to do a line of coke, then lifts her head, focused on Ellis. "You must be the big shot throwing this party," she says.

Ellis turns away from her, shy. Driven by Ellis's ignorance, she saunters over and joins him on the couch. Ellis shifts in his seat, remaining quiet. The woman rests her legs over his lap. "No need to be nervous, sweetie. I just want to have a little fun with you tonight. Don't you want to have fun with me?" she says, caressing Ellis's face.

Ellis chugs a sip of beer. She lowers the bottle from his mouth and places it on the coffee table. Then, she scoots herself onto his lap and kisses him. Ellis's body follows her lead. Walton and Jay leave with Lil in their arms. Clay stays and does another bump, ignoring Ellis and Fran.

Fran stops kissing him, looks Ellis in the eye and gets off his lap. She stands up and leads him to the bed. On his back, she unbuckles his pants, removes them without much assistance, and tosses them on the floor. Then, she pulls his shirt off over his head. He breathes erratically. His body gets warm. He starts sweating. She leans in and plants another kiss on his mouth, reaching her hand into his briefs. "It's okay, sweetie," she reassures. He breathes heavily as she strokes her arm below his waist. "I think you're ready," she says, with a wink.

Fran removes her dress, wearing no bra and white cotton panties. She's slim-built; her inner thigh has a tattoo that reads *Be yourself*. She takes her panties off and drops them on the floor. Ellis barely blinks, studying her body. Clay sits on the couch, watching them.

She climbs on top of Ellis, places his hands on her waist and guides him inside her. His breath increases as her body rocks forward and backward. She picks up speed and her moans get louder. Ellis's body tightens as she sways on top of him, her hair brushing against his face. Faster now, her moans are more intense. His body writhes. He can't control himself and has an orgasm. His body goes limp. Fran slows and kisses him on the forehead. Before either of them can say anything, Clay scoops her up in his arms yelling, "My turn!" She giggles as he carries her to the couch.

Ellis is left alone in bed, naked and curled up in a ball of shame facing the wall, with his back to them. He pulls a pillow over his head to try and block out their sounds. It doesn't work. He hops out of bed, hurries to get his clothes on and darts out the door, running all the way home.

Ellis rushes to his bathroom and vomits into the toilet bowl. After he expels all the beer and bile, he washes out his mouth and examines himself in the mirror. The same but different. He changes into his pajamas and crawls into bed, where he lies with his eyes open, unable to fall asleep. For nearly two hours he stays in this state, staring at the ceiling, while the silence of the room devours him. A knock at the door startles him from his abyss of thoughts. Through the door a muffled voice emerges. "Hey buddy, it's me, Clay! I'm real sorry and just came to make things right."

Ellis gets up and turns on the light. He opens the door. Clay stands in the hallway with Jay and Walton. Jay shoves Ellis into the room, knocking him to the ground. The three men enter. Clay goes straight for the end table and opens the top drawer, removing the mason jar. Ellis scrambles to get up, but Jay kicks him in the face knocking him back down. Walton joins Jay and they hold him down while Clay pockets the cash jar. Then, he approaches Ellis, who helplessly wrestles on the ground. "It's nothing personal, Ellie boy," Clay says before kicking Ellis in the head, knocking him unconscious.

Ellis wakes on the floor of his room in the morning. He gets himself to his feet and slumps into the bathroom. He looks in the mirror. His eye is swollen. Gently, he touches it and winces in pain. His mouth is covered in dry blood. He turns on the faucet and cleans his face. Back in the main room, he begins packing his belongings.

Ellis spends the day moving the few possessions he's acquired into the void. He sets the record player up by the apple tree and stacks the records on the floor beneath it. He empties a backpack full of books and toiletries onto the floor and organizes them. He grabs one of the books, *The Count of Monte Cristo*, and sits down on the ground, leaning against the apple tree. Bullet walks to him and licks the injuries on his face, then settles by his side. No matter how many times Ellis attempts to read, he can't. His concentration keeps wandering past the pages of the book and settling on his rifle, which sits on the floor tucked to the side of the entrance.

of life to be preserved by his aide. No matter what circumstance the

attempt to avoid in vain this dangerous other hand which . . . over

the peril . . . people and . . . rising . . . all . . . on the the

. . . the continue

Rabid Dogs

———— 🍎 ————

Winter 1983

*N*ight has fallen and Ellis crouches on the ground behind the office of the Wayward, peering around the corner of the wall into the parking lot. Sweat collects on his forehead and he grunts from a similar discomfort he received when he was a boy on the outside with Marie. The blips and visions of Bullet return in sporadic fashion. He closes his eyes and rubs them to snap back to reality.

Jay enters the lot in a beat-up sedan. He parks outside a room, gets out and knocks on the door. Clay answers and lets him in. Ellis stays low and stealthily works his way from the office to the motel room door with his rifle over his shoulder. He stands and swings his back to the wall space between the door and the room's window. He peers through the blinds. Clay, Jay, and Walton commiserate around the coffee table with drinks and drugs. Ellis lowers the rifle into his hand and makes sure it's loaded. He knocks on the door. It opens a couple of seconds later and Jay sticks his head out, sprinkles of cocaine residue around his nose. "Back up," Ellis says, pressing the barrel of the gun to Jay's temple.

Clay's snorts can be heard from inside. "Ain't a fuckin' barn man."

Jay slowly steps back into the room with his arms in the air. Clay and Walton stand to attention when they see the gun and throw their hands up. Ellis steps into the room and kicks the door closed behind him. Clay drops his hands in relief. "Oh, it's just you, Ellie boy. Listen, I can explain." He steps closer to Ellis.

Ellis shifts position and draws the gun on Clay, stopping him in his tracks. "My money, I want it back," Ellis demands. He winces from pain in his gut and catches a hallucination of Bullet standing behind Clay. He slaps himself in the face.

"Ellis, no hard feelings. We're sorry. Things got a little out of control, ya know? With the booze, the powder. It happens," Clay says, stepping back as Ellis pushes forward with the barrel between his eyes.

"You two," Ellis instructs Jay and Walton, "Sit on the couch behind Clay." The two men look at each other. "Right now!" Ellis yells.

They take a seat.

Ellis spots the cash on the dresser, next to the TV.

"Get it and bring it to me," he tells Clay.

"Let's take it easy, pal. No trigger fingers necessary," Clay says. He cautiously crosses the room and picks up the money. Ellis steps closer, beads of sweat dripping down his forehead.

"You're in a real pickle here, kid. One I don't think you thought through real well," Clay tells him, signaling to the men on the couch. Walton leaps up and lunges forward for the gun. Ellis reacts in a flash and shoots Walton in the leg, sending him reeling back onto the couch.

Clay and Jay cower in fear. "Okay, okay, take it. Here you go. Take it, ya fucking lunatic!" Clay yells, holding out the money.

Ellis snatches it from his hand and orders Clay and Jay to get to their feet. "You two, come with me. Jay, bring your keys," Ellis says, the rifle still pointed at them.

The three of them exit, leaving Walton behind, who rolls around in pain as he keeps pressure on the hole in his leg. The figment of Bullet watches Ellis exit the room.

***

Jay parks his car at the Western Pass park-and-ride and turns it off. Clay is in the passenger's seat. Ellis, breathing heavier than before, sits behind them with the rifle pointed at Clay's head.

"You okay, Ellie boy?" Clay asks.

"Out," Ellis tells the men.

All three of them exit the vehicle and Ellis leads them into the woods.

"Where ya taking us? Listen, I know we did ya wrong but we can fix this," Clay says, desperation cradling his voice.

"Let us go, you crazy fuck," Jay says. He starts crying.

Ellis doesn't utter a word and keeps leading them forward. Eventually, they reach the clearing and stand before JoJo. Ellis sweeps around them, never lowering the gun, and places his hand over *C.A +* *J.L. 5/13/57*. The doorway opens and both men fall to their knees in awe. Ellis comes back around them with the rifle drawn on their backs and orders them to step inside.

"Listen! We are sorry. We were just trying to see another day. Eat another meal," Clay begs. Ellis pushes the nose of the gun into his back, quieting him.

The men step into the darkness, Ellis in tow. Inside, they survey the rotten scenery. Their eyes land on Bullet, who stands beside the apple tree.

Jay halts dead center in the void. "What the fuck is this?"

"Keep moving," Ellis says, walking them in front of the apple tree. A sense of relief washes over him. He breathes easier with the dissipating pain.

Bullet steps between the two frightened men to join Ellis at their backs. They tremble with fear as the tree throbs and the apples glisten through with a neon yellow.

"This place, I've recently realized, will never let me go. I thought I could run and build a life outside again. Refuse its call to me and fight its sickness. Maybe even make a few friends. But I'm tethered somehow. I see now, it has a job for me. It hungers and I must feed it. It craves a not-too-distant-relative to the fear you feel right now."

The two men breathe nervously as Ellis steps closer.

"Only one of you leaves here tonight. The other gives it what it wants. It's up to you both to decide who that is," Ellis says, ominously.

Clay and Jay turn their heads to face each other, unsure. Jay charges Clay and wraps his hands around his throat before Clay has a chance to react. Clay beats at Jay's arms but, considering Jay's size, it's useless. His fingers press harder around Clay's throat, bringing the suffocating man to his knees. Jay chokes him to the point of nearly passing out and lets go. Then, he quickly runs for the exit, back out into the woods. Clay tries to yell, but the words can't exit his mouth.

Ellis directs Clay to stand up. He does, begging through exasperated breath to be spared. "Please, don't kill me, Ellis. Please."

"I'm not going to kill you," Ellis tells him.

"Then, what are ya going to do?" Clay asks.

"Survive."

Bullet walks to the little apple tree and, from it, steps a woman about Ellis's age. She stares deep into Clay's eyes. Clay recollects who she is. He breaks down.

"No. No. Not you. I am sorry."

She plucks an apple from the tree and carries it to clay.

He weeps yellow tears. "I should've done something. I'm sorry. I was a stupid kid. I was scared of what would happen."

The woman stops his blathering by pressing the apple to his lips. His hand shakes as he takes it from her. His teeth rip a chunk from it. As he swallows, the ecstasy of the taste washes over his face and the bliss mixes with his panic. "I should have stayed. I should have kept them off of you." Clay says to the woman.

Her face sinks into a rage. With one hand she grabs Clay's arm. The other hand grips a branch of the apple tree. They vanish. The tree flickers with light, and color begins to return to Ellis's surroundings. The doorway closes back up. Ellis drops the rifle to the ground and walks to the record player. He puts on *Duke* by Genesis. The opening song "Behind the Lines" begins. Ellis joins Bullet on the ground by the apple tree with *The Count of Monte Cristo*. He opens it and reads.

Under the Skin

Winter 2031

*F*rank lays on the couch in the living room, visibly rattled, but no longer yelling. Laura sits next to him, stroking his forehead. "Laura, you can't go back to that horrible place," he says. Laura listens but doesn't reply. Frank doubles down. "You're not going back there."

"We can talk about this in the morning. You need to rest," Laura says, almost in a whisper.

"I forbid you from going to that place again."

Laura's had enough. "You can't stop me from going there. I need that place, Frank. I know tonight was a lot."

Frank bolts up from the couch. "Do you know, Laura? Really? A lot? Did you get visited by some fucking distorted version of a monster that used to lock you in closets and swing the buckle end of a belt at your head?!"

"No, I didn't. And I'm sorry that you did, Frank." Laura stands up from the couch to join him at the center of the room. She places a hand on his cheek. "You've worked so hard to get through those horrors and I will forever be proud of you for that. I would do anything to rewind what occurred back there for you; but for me, bubba is there. I need him."

Frank's face sinks. "I understand the desire to go back. You think I wouldn't spend every second with him if I could? But that's not him, and I fear for you."

"Don't make this difficult," she says.

"You keep going there and you'll lose me. Forever," Frank replies.

Laura's hand drifts away from Frank's face. "I already have."

She swallows the truth of the statement like a sharpened knife. The words sever whatever remaining, frayed strands that once knotted them together in the universe. Frank doesn't respond. With the uncomfortable silence in tow, he leaves the room.

Laura sits back down on the couch. The room is quiet. She leans her head back across the top of the couch and stares at the ceiling. A deep breath fills her chest as tears break from her eyes and fall down the sides of her face.

***

Ellis, full of rage, looks upon the ground with his hands clenched into tight fists. His eyes follow the rot lines that run throughout the void. Venom in its veins.

Bullet sits at the base of the apple tree, undisturbed. Ellis awaits an answer that never comes. His frustration grows.

"He didn't deserve that."

The deer remains quiet in mind and unmoved from its comfort.

"Speak, or I'll destroy this place!"

Ellis frantically tumbles about, wrecking and distorting the surroundings. He renders the once beautiful landscapes into abstract splashes of color. His hands wipe with fury until nothing is recognizable.

132

"Speak, or I'll destroy us!"

Again, his threats bounce off Bullet.

He charges the deer, arms spread like wings, eradicating all that rests on either side of his fingertips. His hands are covered and drip with a putrid brown. He raises his fists, locked in concentration on the unfazed animal. His body billows with anger. Releasing a primal roar, his breaths of fire sift through his teeth and out into the world. When his lungs finish emptying their rage, he lowers his hands and falls to his knees, defeated.

"You don't know anything," he remarks to Bullet.

The two of them sit alone in the wake of Ellis's destruction. JoJo, twisted in turmoil, an abstract painting floating through liminal space, somehow managing to hold hints of beauty in its disarray.

***

In the shower, Frank washes himself as if he's not just trying to scrub the day off his skin, but from his very soul. He rigorously cleans the place where his father had touched him, to the point his shoulder begins to bleed. Several old scars are visible across his back. He uses a touch screen in the wall before him to gradually raise the water temperature, scolding himself away from unwanted feelings. The tension in his body rises with the heat, until he can no longer take it and turns the water off.

He steps from the shower and into a cloud of steam that's filled the bathroom. Through the fog, his reflection in the mirror is nearly pitch black. Closer now, he sees it is his father, as he was in the void, staring at him from the murky glass. Frank is startled and closes his eyes hard, repeating, "No." He opens them back up.

His father is still there, staring at him, unblinking, and smiling cruelly at his torment. Sr.'s hand reaches out for him and touches the opposite side of the glass, unable to exit. Frank cautiously approaches to get a better look. He edges closer and uses his hand to wipe away the remains of the moisture, circling his palm over the section his father occupies. Frank Sr. lunges forward and starts clawing frantically from behind the glass.

Frank has had enough and darts away, slamming the door behind him. He sits on the edge of the bed in the guest bedroom, naked and wet. He shakes his head to try and get his mind straight. He slows his breathing and then notices something on the palm of the hand he used to wipe the mirror. He moves it under the bedside lamp to get a better look. The veins are darker than usual, almost black, glowing when the light catches them right. He wipes at them with his opposing thumb. It isn't dirt. It is under the skin.

Lovers' Picnic

Spring/Summer 1963

*E*llis, a boy, lies in purple grass, his flesh glittered with a pink glow from a sun constructed within the void. Bullet sits by his side, his head cozied across Ellis's legs. The void is filled with colors of no specific form or landscape; greens, reds, yellows fade in and out of one another. Bullet lifts his inquisitive head and flutters his eyes in the direction of the window at the exit. The deer grows more curious and stands.

"What's the fuss?" asks Ellis, not expecting an answer.

Bullet walks toward the exit to stare out into the clearing. Ellis begrudgingly gets up and joins. In the fresh green grass outside their prison, a young couple sits on a picnic blanket, surrounded by a fully bloomed forest during late spring. The woman is fair skinned, with cherub pink cheeks, dressed in a flowered romper and big, bug-eyed sunglasses. Her long, red hair dances in the subtle breeze. Her skin shines under the orange sunlight, the freckles on her face bright and visible from the tree.

In front of her sits a man, darker in complexion. He wears comfortable denim jeans and a plain white t-shirt, exposing his well-built muscular frame. His clean-shaven face reveals a strong jawline. The hair on his head is cut close to his scalp, and his soft eyes only focus on her.

The man empties a knapsack of sandwiches and assorted snacks onto their picnic blanket. She picks up an apple slice and holds it to her upper lip like a mustache, mouthing something that makes them laugh. The man snatches the apple slice from her hand and gobbles it up. She playfully slaps his shoulder. He leans in and breaks the flirtation with a kiss. After their lips part, they hold each other in their sights for a moment. She pulls her hair behind her ears and gives the man a bashful smile.

He pulls out a small radio and turns it on, placing it on the corner of the blanket to enjoy songs Ellis and Bullet can't hear. She unwraps their sandwiches and hands one to the man while mumbling a few lyrics to herself. They spend most of the afternoon bobbing their heads along to the music while they read, offering fruit to each other in between chapters. Occasionally, they make out, always stopping to gain composure before things get too heavy.

The woman reacts to whatever song starts playing and turns the dial up on the radio. Then, she stands and dances barefoot, the blades of grass tangling around her toes. The man lowers his book to watch her. She says something and they laugh. Holding out her arms for him to join her, he refuses at first, but she insists and pulls him to his feet. She leads and he awkwardly sways to mimic her motions. As their dancing slows, the man looks directly at the giant oak tree, as if he spotted Ellis watching them from the other side.

Ellis perks up and bangs on the inside of the tree to get the man's attention. Green dust escapes his mouth with each scream. The man grabs the woman's hand and leads her to the tree.

"Hello. I'm here," Ellis yells, banging more aggressively.

The couple stands before the tree. The man pulls out a pocketknife and opens it. Then, he proceeds to carve something into the bark; neither noticing the desperate boy trapped inside the tree. Ellis slumps in defeat.

The man finishes what he started and closes the knife, returning it to his pocket. The woman extends her hand and settles her fingertips on the carving. The couple admire the display and kiss. He pulls her closer. She drapes her arms upon his shoulders, clasping her hands behind his neck. Again, they kiss. When their mouths release, she checks the time on her wristwatch and the two of them panic, hurrying to collect their belongings and leave.

A week later, the couple returns. And, a week after that. Nearly every week for the duration of the warm weather, they find themselves back there, with their blanket and their radio and their books. Ellis and Bullet remain glued to the couple each time they return.

One day, the woman lowers her book after only reading a couple of pages. The man peers up from his. She takes it out of his hand and puts it down by hers. She runs her finger up her arm and removes the shoulder strap of her top and pulls him in by the collar for a kiss. He tilts his head to place his mouth on her shoulder. Then, moves to her neck. She runs her hands through his hair and claws his shirt off over his head. He helps her remove her shirt and then her bra. He gently lowers her to the blanket, shifting his weight on top of her. They kiss like wild animals, groping clumsily to help each other out of the rest of their clothes. Her legs wrap around his waist as he thrusts forward. Her eyes shut, closing tighter with every forward motion of the man's body. Their chests heave heavier and faster with each passing second. Their bodies become one rhythmic mass of flesh. Her mouth points wide-open to the sky, as if she were ready to swallow the universe.

Ellis barely blinks as he watches them make love. He squirms in place, folding one leg over another to suppress his bodily reaction to what their lovemaking stirs in him. His face grows concerned as he presses down on his lap with his hand to try and make his arousal go away. It doesn't. He panics and retreats to his patch of grass, cradling into a ball. On the verge of tears, his breath works overtime. He scrunches himself tighter and tighter. It takes several minutes for him to calm himself and, when he does, he rolls over to his back; eyes locked on the waves of color that fill the void. Floating gardens and mystical looking upside-down hills are painted across the surface above him. He remains in that position for almost an hour, before returning to the exit to see if the couple is still there. They are not. Summer turns to fall. Fall to winter. Winter to spring. They never return.

Existence Absent

Winter 2031

*L*aura, visibly unnerved by the extra stillness of the woods that morning, traipses along the path she has walked several times before. The breeze, extra vicious off the stream, takes her breath away. JoJo stands in the clearing, looking more treacherous against a soulless sky blanketed in gray. There is no opening. No sign of Ellis or Bullet.

Laura bangs on the trunk of the tree. Ellis watches her from where he sits. He does his best to ignore her, but it's impossible to. A voyeur, he walks to the window and spends a few moments in observation, transfixed on her eyes.

He opens the doorway. Laura is surprised by the disheveled and incomprehensible patterns that cover the interior. Ellis's anger can be seen in every crevice. She walks to him and looks in his eyes. The tension coils in the shortened distance between them. To his surprise, she moves closer and hugs him. Goosebumps spring up on his skin.

He smells the crux of her neck and the laces of hair that brush against his face. His breath deepens against her skin. She squeezes him a bit tighter, forcing him to raise his arms and hug her back.

"I'm sorry for what happened to your husband. I've never seen anything like that before," Ellis admits.

"I believe you."

Through a watered blur she can see Billy's small frame behind Ellis. She lets go and runs towards Billy, falling to her knees, to pull him into her body. Billy reaches one of his hands to her eyes. His little fingers wipe the sadness from her face and use it to start building along the ground. He makes a small purple garden and then hurries back to remove more color from Laura's cheeks. He follows the garden up with a stream. Then, a small mountain to neighbor the stream.

He nudges Ellis to bend down so he can grab whatever residue from his mother's eyes collected on the shoulder of his sweater. The boy carves out a big enough area for the three of them to lie down and look up into the void. Laura watches as the two of them draw her an existence absent of the one she walked away from. Ellis uses the tip of his pointer finger to blot multicolored stars into the black canvas. Billy constructs a crescent moon as red as the devil to accompany the stars.

Billy tugs on Laura's shirt. He points ahead, towards Bullet, who sits in his usual spot at the base of the apple tree; his charcoal eyes standing out in the sea of color. Ellis waves Bullet over. The deer begrudgingly joins them and nestles up by their feet. Billy pets it, stroking the skin between its eyes and encourages Laura to join in. He takes her hand and places it on the deer's body. It is smooth and slick with what she can only describe as, "Mini thunderstorms traveling around my fingers."

"For this place to exist, Bullet must exist," Ellis says. More somberly he follows up with, "For him to exist, I must exist." His eyes plead for freedom, but Ellis forces a smile and changes the subject. "So, what should we create next?"

Routine Protocol

Winter 1999

Decrepit landscapes cover every inch of the void. An adult Ellis sits naked, leisurely turning the pages of *Cujo* while Love's *Reel to Real* spins on the record player. He finishes the sentence he's on and smacks the book shut. In the thick of the darkness lies a dim patch of grass, where Bullet rests; a faltering sun casts a depleted ray of light across the deer's face. Ellis's body cuts in and out of the light, occasionally eclipsing his companion, as he now paces the void, reciting the book from memory:

> *"It would, perhaps, not be amiss to point out that he had always tried to be a good dog. He had tried to do all the things his MAN and his WOMAN, and most of all his BOY, had asked or expected of him. He would have died for them, if that had been required. He had never wanted to kill anybody. He*

had been struck by something, possibly destiny, or fate, or only a degenerative nerve disease called rabies. Free will was not a factor."

The remaining tint of the sun vanishes and the gateway to the void melts away and opens. Ellis finishes another few sentences of the book out loud, then rummages through a pile of clothes. He takes his time getting dressed. He picks up a backpack and stuffs some books into it. Bullet nudges his arm. Ellis gives him a gentle stroke on the head.

"Be back soon."

The trees are barren. Dead leaves crunch beneath his feet. A bird sings in the distance, while the footsteps of smaller animals can be heard rustling nearby. Ellis walks along disinterested. No cars populate the Western Pass park-and-ride when he exits the woods. He peers across the road to where the cliffside kisses the sky. Gray clouds lurch, keeping the sun hidden and the morning darker than it should be.

Nobody is in the cemetery when he arrives. He kneels before his father's gravestone in quiet observation. It's chipped in several places and stained with time. A stark difference between it and the ones surrounding it. The visit only lasts a few minutes. A quiet goodbye and into town he goes.

Ellis idles on the steps of the local library. A group of teenagers exit and pass him, paying him no mind. One wears a tight nylon dress and fluffy, green boots. Another, in loose fitting jeans and a wrinkled leather jacket; his hair taut and tall in the form of a mohawk. Ellis stares a bit longer than he should. The boy notices. "Why don't you take a picture, asshole?"

Ellis promptly diverts his attention away from them and onto the newspaper stand right behind the library doors. He enters and checks the date on one of the papers: *November 15th, 1999.*

He heads to the return desk, watching an older woman stack

records into nearby crates.

"Hello there," Ellis remarks loud enough to gain her attention.

"Oh, hello dear," she says, walking towards him. Her gray hair sprouts from the corners of her head. "How can I help you?"

Ellis removes his backpack, takes several stacks of books from it, and places them on the countertop before the librarian. "I have returns."

"I'd say so," she replies. She opens a book to remove the checkout card and scan it with a handheld device, surprised to see it has a handwritten card in it. She examines a few more of the books. The same style card sits in the front covers. "Sir, these books were last checked out in 1983. I wouldn't even know where to begin with the amount of late fees owed."

Ellis plays to her sympathy. "I found them in my mother's house. She's no longer with us."

"Well, in that case, we will just forget about those pesky fees. Sorry for your loss."

"Thank you."

The remainder of his morning is spent making exhaustive choices. Carefully, Ellis scans every shelf, thumbing through books to see which catch his eye. He sets his new pile down on the librarian's counter and then thumbs through the record crates, taking what strikes his fancy. She walks him through how to sign up for a library card and scans his choices. One-by-one Ellis fills his backpack up with the new reads.

"Maybe try and bring these back in the current decade," the librarian jokes.

"Can't make any promises," he says.

***

Ellis spends the early afternoon at Kentwood Park. He makes himself comfortable on a bench near the very spot Marie took him on a picnic. He passes time between reading from one of his new books,

Holes, and devouring a giant roast beef and provolone sandwich. A few stragglers make their way through the park while he's there: dog walkers, joggers, and a couple using the park as a shortcut to the other side of town. After a handful of chapters, he packs his things up and continues on before the cold becomes unbearable.

***

He stops at his childhood home. It is still new and vibrant and vastly unfamiliar. The door is painted green and the house cream, which went well with the garden in front of it. Ellis remains on the sidewalk. His sights roam upwards, past the roof, to the naked tree in the backyard, its fingers breaching the skyline. He moves a few feet down the sidewalk, in front of the driveway, to get a better glimpse of the backyard. The tree is massive and majestic, its trunk oak-brown and primitive. It is more mature than the last time he saw it; more wrinkled from the cycle of seasons he's missed in the outside world.

A car horn startles him. Ellis does an about face. A middle-aged, black woman idles in a BMW sedan. He moves out of the way and the car pulls into the driveway. By the time the woman exits the vehicle to acknowledge Ellis, he is halfway down the street.

Hunting Grounds

Winter 1999

*R*ebels is mostly empty, except for a few afternoon regulars. A jittery, disheveled man hassles the bartender over some change.

"Stop busting my balls, Moo. It's all there," the bartender says.

"It better be. Last time you stole two dollars from me," Moo says. He stuffs the money into his pants pocket.

"No way," Ellis whispers to himself as Moo passes.

"Can I help you?" Moo asks, disgruntled.

Ellis shakes his head.

"Everyone's got a fucking staring problem nowadays."

The bartender acknowledges Ellis's presence and yells, "Pay him no mind. What can I get ya?"

Ellis approaches the bar. "I'll have a coke."

"Usually, people want something in the coke, but okay."

The bartender scoops a few ice cubes into a glass, using the bar gun to squirt it full of soda. Ellis places money on the bar top and grabs his drink. He makes his way to the back of the room and places his belongings down on a table near the jukebox. Then, he proceeds to the bathroom.

He relieves himself at the urinal farthest from the only other man in there, who struggles to keep himself up while he pees. His jeans are caked with dirt. He can barely keep them up along his waist. The flannel shirt he has on is frayed along the bottom seams, with a widening hole over one elbow. The greasy brown hair on his head reaches halfway down his back. He turns to his side and notices Ellis's eyes fixated on him but doesn't say anything. Ellis finishes up, flushes, and heads to the sink. While washing his hands, the man at the urinal struggles fastening his belt and stumbles backwards into a stall.

"You okay?" Ellis hurries to help him.

"Slipped on the fuckin' tile. Always goddamn moppin' in here," the man says.

Ellis helps him to his feet and the two men exit back into the bar.

"Who are you here with?" Ellis asks.

"I keep my own company, kid," the man replies, his breath reeking of stale beer.

"You're more than welcome to join me over there," Ellis says, pointing at the table where his soda awaits.

Ellis sits the man down at the table and asks, "You want something to drink?"

"Jack soda," the man commands.

Ellis goes to the bar, orders the drink, and brings it back to the man. "You like music?" Ellis asks in between sips of his soda.

"Who doesn't?"

The jukebox is clean. The glass display is pristine and easy to see through. Ellis selects "Leaving on a Jet Plane".

"Fuckin' folk, blah," the man mutters.

Ellis laughs, accompanying him at the table. "What would you have preferred?"

"Blues. The only music that tells the goddamn truth." The man holds his drink up. Ellis clinks glasses with him and they both take a sip, uttering a "Cheers" under their breath.

"What even is the truth?" Ellis prods.

"That heavy wave that knocks you on your ass. Carrying all types of regret and wrong turns. It's pain, my man."

"What kind of pain?"

The man smirks. "Every kind, my man. Every. Fucking. Kind."

***

The sun is setting as the two men walk along the edge of town. The man exclaims his excitement for a warm bed and hot meal. However, he begins to question it the more distance they put between themselves and the last house they passed.

"It isn't much further from here," Ellis says.

Puzzled, the man asks, "You live out here?"

Ellis decides to lie. "I told you. It's no ordinary place. My family, they have a cabin."

The man remains on the other side of the trees, in the Western Pass park-and-ride.

Ellis plays to his vices. "I make a mean stew and I've got a bottle with your name on it just waiting to be opened."

It works. The man follows him through the woods and into the clearing, where no such cabin exists.

"Don't be nervous about what you're going to see," Ellis warns him.

The man stiffens in apprehension, his breath stuck in his throat, as Ellis places his hand on the tree and the doorway opens.

"I promise you. What lies in there is better than what haunts you out here. Welcome to JoJo, a place where truth can become something beautiful," Ellis preaches.

The man steps inside behind Ellis. Everything is dark. Ellis's record player and a pile of clothes sit in the middle distance. Beyond that, Bullet approaches the two men from the dilapidated apple tree with his beating heart pulsing through the blackness of his exterior.

"What is this place?" the man asks, the cold air leaving his lungs in mystical, blue dust. He reaches his hand out to touch it and the neon particles flutter away.

The apple tree ripples with color and out steps the silhouette of an older woman. She is short and stout, her hair draped over her shoulders. Her colorless dress is hard to discern over her pale, wrinkled skin. "Momma," the man says. More particles of his breath take shape in arbitrary hues. The dust floats her way and fills her body with color. "How? How are you here?" the man asks. He hesitates to take a step forward. "How is she here?"

"It's okay. Go to her," Ellis says.

The mother plucks a golden apple and hands it to the man.

"Go ahead," Ellis says

The man bites into the apple and sighs with delight at the taste. "Momma, your macaroni!"

Candy coated tears collect on the man's face as he falls into his mother's arms. She kisses him on the cheek and leads him to the apple tree. They both vanish into the unknown. Color rebounds. The void is alive again. Ellis has paid his dues. He closes the doorway, puts on a Fleetwood Mac vinyl, and begins crafting landscapes from the scattered iridescence at his fingertips.

Father Figure

Winter 2031

*I*t's late morning in the Nagan household. The air hangs stale and stuffy while the floorboard heater hums amongst the quiet of the guest bedroom. Frank is asleep in a pool of sweat, his chest thumping up and down with heavy breaths. His father watches him from a mirror attached to a bureau across the room. The contained rage of his reflection permeates the atmosphere; a marionette of darkness salivating over the strings that control Frank's waking life. A cell phone vibrates on the nightstand. Frank struggles to wake and assimilates to being conscious, realizing what time it is. He picks up the phone, his sweaty hands trembling, and answers it.

"Good morning, sir," says Maisy from the other side, her voice flat.

"Screw the pleasantries," Frank gruffs. "What is it?"

"Mr. Billips has been calling about the repair on his property."

"He should just calm the fuck down," Frank snaps, shocking himself, and hangs up the call before Maisy can respond.

He forces himself up and sits on the edge of the bed. "It was all a nightmare. A bad nightmare," he assures himself. But the dark veins on his hands tell him otherwise.

He heads into the bathroom towards the sink but stops short when he sees his father in the glass. Sr. punches from behind the mirror; a wicked smile curdles his lips. Frank quickly turns around in a panic.

Back in the bedroom, Frank gathers his clothes and notices his father in the bureau. Then, he sees him faintly in the windows. His father even watches him from the monitor of a turned off TV mounted on the wall. Frank fights the urge to face the morbid reflections. He works fast to get his clothes on with his eyes closed. Telepathically, his father finds a way in. "Destroy Laura's paintings. Burn the house down when she's home."

Frank buttons his pants and presses his hands against his ears as he exits into the downstairs hallway. His father taunts him from every frame hanging on the walls, his gray-scale face overlapping those of the family photos. "Hold your hand to a lit stove, you weak, pathetic excuse for a man." The words burrow past Frank's hands.

Sr. is everywhere he is. He is every image on every surface that can reflect one, even on the windows of Frank's truck when he leaves the house. "Hang the neighbor's dog in front of them," his father taunts.

His disfigured visage is waiting for Frank in the rear-view mirror, prodding his mind as he drives. "Do us all a favor and drive off the road."

Even at the store, in the broken SuperMart sign, his father stares menacingly, clawing at the glass, fighting to reach him. Frank can't help but fall into a trance at his father's impression in the shattered covering of the sign's letters. Sr. continues to speak to him subconsciously, trying to plant dark seeds in his mind. "Give in and punish everyone. Become your legacy - a plague. End your miserable life and fade into the forgotten bowels of time, where you belong."

Frank closes his eyes, concentrating on ignoring the voice. His father's words rake against his skull. "You weren't meant to exist in the first place."

Frank's breathing increases. His hands quiver.

"You could've come in first and said howdy before getting to work, Frank," Mr. Billips says, interrupting his spell.

Frank stands and doesn't say anything, focusing on burying his father's fight for control.

"Pull some glass from the sign and slit his throat," Sr. goads.

Frank ignores the thought.

Mr. Billips takes note of the day-old stubble creeping onto Frank's typically clean-shaven face. He extends a hand out to his old friend. "How goes it?"

Frank hesitates and looks back to his father's face locked onto him, cold and unrelenting.

"Frank...," Mr. Billips calls out, his hand still in the air waiting to be greeted.

Frank shuts his eyes harder, trying to push the nightmare away.

"Frank, you okay there, buddy?"

Frank turns back and snaps himself out of it enough to raise his hand and greet the man. Mr. Billips spots the blackened veins in Frank's hands. Then, he sees a bit of it creeping out from under Frank's collar. Discreetly, he wipes his hand inside his coat pocket. "How are you feeling today, Frank? Everything alright?"

"Oh yeah, yeah!" Frank mumbles, scratching the darkened veins on his neck.

"You don't look well."

"I'm fine," Frank reassures.

"I know it's been a little rough on your family lately. Why don't you take a couple of days off?"

Sr. scratches at every reflective surface around them simultaneously. Frank can't hold back his father's fury anymore. "I'm fucking fine. Now stop asking and let me fix your goddamned, too-low-hanging, cheap shit sign, alright?"

Incensed by Frank's demeanor, Mr. Billips charges back. "You shouldn't speak to your customers like that."

"Why do you care how I am?"

A few people in the parking lot pause to observe the commotion between the two men.

"Now, it's clear something is going on with you, Frank. But I won't be disrespected. Take the day and get yourself checked out before this gets any uglier."

Skin reddened with anger, Frank breaks a piece of glass free from the sign and approaches Mr. Billips. He gets uncomfortably close, causing Brian to stiffen up. Sr. devilishly smirks around the two men. Frank grips the glass hard, fighting his anger, aiming to keep his hand from raising it. Blood begins to seep from his balled fist and down the edge of the shard.

Frank, uncompromising, leers at the frightened store owner. His eyes fill with the same poison that's replaced his blood. The sight causes Mr. Billips to gasp. Both men are locked in the fever-pitched tension between them. Frank leans in a bit closer. A vindictive smile, mimicking his father's, grows across his lips. Condescendingly, he laughs directly in Mr. Billips' face, his hot breath backing the man up. Frank scowls and drops the glass on the ground, heading back to his truck. He keeps his gaze fixed to his feet, avoiding his father as best he can.

He unlocks the truck and gets in, his breathing both laborious and angry. Sr. greets him in the rearview mirror. Frank is transfixed by his father's eyes. Sr. nods in cruel approval. Frank floors the gas pedal in the direction of Mr. Billips, narrowly missing him, and crashes directly into the sign, destroying it. The impact is enough to cause him to slam his head against the steering wheel and split the skin of his forehead.

Mr. Billips gets to his feet, astonished.

Frank lowers the passenger side window and howls, "Fix it yourself, Brian."

He backs his truck up, the front end gnarled, and exits the parking lot, peeling off into traffic; all but causing an accident with oncoming motorists. Increasing in speed, he drives until he is out of the downtown area and alone on a rural roadway. Lost in the death of his father's glare, Frank pays little mind to where he's going. The yellow lines blur into one as his tires violently spin him deeper down the thin stretch of pavement - deeper into his madness.

Something grabs his attention. The elder's hold breaks. He pulls off to the side of the road and brings the truck to a stop. On the floor, below the passenger's seat, is Billy's toy plane. Hands shaking, he reaches down and picks it up. He holds it in his lap. Then, raises it closer to his face, his eyes drowning in what he no longer has. With his other hand, he balls a fist and furiously punches the steering wheel, wailing guttural sounds of grief. Punched out, he lowers his head, exhausted and despondent. Waiting for him when he sits back up is the relentless focus of the monster he can't seem to escape. Sr. lurks in the windshield, his eyes moving from Frank to the plane. "No! It's mine!" Frank shouts.

The monster's stare drifts from the plane to a cliff on the other side of the guardrail. Frank can't resist his father's grip. The plane releases from his hand and he exits the truck, wrestling with his own muscles as they force him through a small clearing, to the cliff. He peers over the edge. About a hundred feet below, a calm body of water reflects a giant image of his father on the surface, his tentacles thrashing behind him. Sr. gives a wink and a nod to Frank as he teeters above. "No, please!" Frank's feet work against him; his toes are dangling off the edge. Unable to free himself from the poisonous clasp of his past, Frank plummets into the water.

Poisoned Through

Winter 2031

Laura, Ellis, and Billy have turned the void into a decadent tomb of imagination. There isn't a single speck of black left to the human eye. Billy plays under the apple tree, making balls out of the blue mud on the ground. Ellis and Laura sit in the shade, watching a green sun ripple against a chartreuse sky.

"It's unfair," Laura decries.

"What is?" Ellis asks.

"That all this," Laura scans their surroundings, "won't be enough to set you free."

Silence overwhelms them. Ellis sits with a lump in his throat.

"Do you have to feed someone to it?"

Ellis affirms, a sullen look upon his face.

"There's got to be something we can do," Laura says.

Ellis ignores Laura's insistence. "Winter is creeping closer to its end. You should focus on Billy, not me."

"You're too good, Ellis," she says, endearingly.

"No, I'm just trying to be better than I used to be."

"Don't be so hard on yourself," Laura suggests, resting her head on his shoulder.

Ellis's body straightens, taught at the physical contact. Evidently nervous, he stands up and heads for his pile of books. "Want to read for a bit?" he proposes, hardly capable of burying the jitter in his voice.

Laura sits, uncertain. Then, eases herself to her feet. "It's getting a bit late, Ellis. I better go. I should check on Frank."

Ellis holds *The Time Machine*, futzing with the dog ear on the cover, his concentration directed at the ground. Laura ambles over and bundles him up in her arms, squeezing tight. He lets the book go and reciprocates, placing his hands upon her back. With his head nestled in her neck, he breathes heavily. Laura pivots her head and plants a gentle kiss on his cheek. Her lips peel from his skin and she whispers into his ear, "You are not alone."

***

Back home, Laura pulls in behind a police car in the driveway. Deputies Parsons and Mattison are illuminated in her headlights at the front door. Frank's truck is not there. She gets out of her car and walks over to them. "Hi, officers. I promise I was just with a friend. I can give my husband a call if he's out looking for me," she avows.

"Maybe we should go inside first, Mrs. Nagan," Deputy Parsons suggests.

Laura becomes concerned and lets them in, setting her belongings down on a nearby table. "Could I offer either of you a glass of water or something?"

"No, thanks, Mrs. Nagan," Deputy Parsons comments, "Best we get to why we are here."

Laura takes a seat on the couch opposite them. "What is it?"

"Your husband, he had a bizarre altercation with one of his

clients today. Mr. Brian Billips," Deputy Mattison explains.

Laura leans forward, confused. "What kind of altercation?"

"It seems things got heated and threatening. Mr. Billips isn't pressing charges. He called us out of concern," Deputy Parsons states.

Deputy Mattison chimes in. "Mr. Billips said your husband seemed ill, physically and mentally. That he wasn't himself."

"Neither of us have been ourselves," Laura says.

"There's more," Deputy Parsons adds, "his truck was found banged up on the side of the road, by Western Pass. We have a few patrols looking for him."

Laura fights to keep composure and removes her phone from her pocket to dial Frank. It goes straight to his voicemail.

"He's not the type," she tells them; the irony of the situation not escaping her.

"That's a good thing, Mrs. Nagan," Deputy Parsons continues, "Maybe he wandered off somewhere else after. Do you have any idea where he could be?"

***

The patrol car pulls into the cemetery entrance and slinks down the main roadway. Laura sits in the back, giving directions to Deputy Parsons as she drives. They come to a stop in a roundabout and get out. Laura points down a row of tombstones. "This way."

With flashlights in hand, the three of them search, calling out for Frank. It is quiet and cold. The ground is hard under their feet, as if it borrowed rigor mortis from the corpses beneath it. The graveyard's darkness rests eerily around their beams of light. A few steps down an adjacent row of graves Deputy Parsons reveals a hunched over body in her spotlight.

"Frank!" Laura runs to him.

Frank is on his knees, babbling nonsense to Billy's grave, the toy plane atop the tombstone. He is inconsolable and difficult to understand. The only distinct sound is their son's name over and over in between mumbled apologies. Laura rubs his back to keep him warm.

"Frank, it's gonna be okay!"

He is soaking wet to the touch and has yet to acknowledge her presence. The deputies catch up and shine the light on his face, which, to their amazement, is poisoned through, as if black worms traded places with his blood. Deputy Mattison radios for an ambulance, while Deputy Parsons attempts to console the couple.

Upside Down

Summer 1946

*E*llis sits alone on the couch, reading *The Little Island* by Margaret Wise Brown. His joy paves a subtle smile across his face as he scans the lines on the page. The clock on the wall ticks past 9:35 PM. A crescent moon sits high and bright in the clear night sky outside the window behind him. Jazz wafts from a radio on an end table in the living room. His eyes grow heavy. He lets out a massive yawn, dog ears the page, and closes the book, setting it down next to the radio. He slides himself off the couch, walks to the window closest to the front door, pushes back the curtain, and glances outside. The lawn is overgrown. The driveway is empty. Crickets chirp from unknown locations in the darkness. He lets the curtain fall back into place.

He heads to the kitchen, quietly observing his mother's urn above the fireplace as he passes it. At the stove, Ellis stands on a stool and turns on one of the burners to boil water. He hops off the stool and searches through a pantry, removing a box of pasta. Once the water is boiling, he dumps the pasta into the pot, placing the empty box down next to the stove.

He opens the refrigerator. It is mostly empty except for beer and random leftovers. One of the cans of beer is open. Ellis looks over his shoulder to the front door, then back to the open can. He takes it out and smells it at the opening. The pungent aroma makes him wince. He swigs a small sip, immediately repulses, and puts the can back where he found it. Then, hustles to the sink to fill a glass with water, chugging it hastily to wash the beer's aftertaste away. He places the empty glass in the sink and sets the kitchen table, clearing away unread mail and an ashtray full of cigar butts. He serves himself the finished pasta, slathers it with butter, and eats alone.

Upon finishing, Ellis cleans up after himself and washes the dishes. Next, he turns off the radio and lights in the living room. On his way upstairs, through a kitchen window, he sees the shed in the backyard is open.

With a lantern in hand, he traverses the darkness of the backyard, past the tree, and up to the shed. Illuminated at the edge of the lantern's glow is the snout and eyes of an animal. Ellis tiptoes closer. The carcass of a deer hanging upside down comes into full view. Hooks are gouged into its hind legs. Its belly is flayed open, the guts removed. Blood patiently drips from the lifeless tongue dangling out of its mouth into a bucket below. Ellis holds the lantern out further to investigate the bucket. A dark, black pool stares back. He lifts the lantern to the deer's face. Its eyes match the blood in the bucket. Something stirs in the back of the shed. He repositions the light at the sound. A raccoon darts out past him. Ellis recoils in fear, tumbling to the ground.

He gets up, swiftly slams the shed door shut, and rushes back to the house. He locks the back door and catches his breath in the kitchen. Upstairs, he gets into bed fully clothed, with the lights on. Tightly bundled under the blankets on his bed, he lies frightened.

A Desire to Live

Winter 2031

*L*aura sits in the hospital waiting room, holding the toy plane; a small number of people occupy seats around her. One frazzled woman nurses a baby as she attempts to keep her toddler in the seat next to her. The girl fidgets from boredom, not wanting to play with her handheld gaming device any longer. A younger couple is parked against the wall closest to the exit. The man whispers urgent words on his cell phone while the woman sleeps upon his shoulder. Laura shifts in her chair, tapping her feet against the linoleum floor. "Mrs. Nagan," a tall, blonde doctor says from the doorway. Laura springs to her feet and follows the woman into the hallway.

The doctor's demeanor is steady and calm. "Your husband is in stable condition. We gave him a sedative to calm his nerves, but we need to run some more tests to get to the bottom of this. He seems to be dealing with a blood condition that is fast moving. Frankly, it's a testament to his strength that he was able to walk as far as he did," she says.

"Can I see him?" Laura asks.

"Yes, but keep in mind he will need his rest."

***

Frank lies in bed, answering Deputy Parsons and Mattison's questions. He offers very little information to go along with what they already know about the happenings of his day.

"It's all been too much lately, officers. I finally burst. Between my son and whatever the hell has me sick," he analyzes the black lines under his skin, "I was terrified and took it out on a good man. Please give my sincere apologies to Brian if you speak with him again."

The doctor leads Laura into the room.

"Mr. Nagan, that's enough for now. We will give you some time with your wife and be back with any follow-ups tomorrow," Deputy Parsons says.

"Thank you. I am indebted to your service," Frank says.

Laura and the deputies exchange a wordless goodbye. The doctor reminds Laura of the visiting hours and leaves.

Frank pulls Laura in, blurting out, "Laura, I...I can't escape him. He's everywhere, in everything." Frank points to the window. "He's right there."

Sr. silently taunts his son from the window.

Laura checks. The window is empty. "Frank, I don't see anything."

Frank pushes a button on a remote and raises the bed to lean in closer. He whispers, "He's not just there, but in here." Frank points to the black webs growing under his skin. "He wants me to do awful things for him."

"What are you talking about?" Laura asks.

The fear rises in Frank's voice. "I think my father, or at least a part of him, escaped the other day from that place. And he's been

164

following me since, wanting me to hurt people...and myself."

Frank recounts the scene in the parking lot with Mr. Billips, the hellish drive into chaos, and the cliff side, to bring Laura up to speed.

"When I was in the water, I could feel it all around me. A strangle for his control over my body. But then, I thought of Billy... and you-", a meager smile cracks through the horror, "and in that moment, I knew that I couldn't give in. I felt as if my lungs were about to burst, but I had to fight my way to the surface. I swam with everything I had." Frank pauses, distracted by Sr.'s sneering grimace in the window; a grayscale monster shadowed by the wild swing of its tentacles. Without looking away, he continues, "He was watching from the surface, still holding on, furious that I escaped."

Laura listens attentively, taking another glance at the window only to find it empty still.

"I ran, knowing there was only one place I wanted to be...one place I needed to be. At the cemetery, I wouldn't be under the weight of the evil spell in that bastard's eyes!"

Laura places the toy plane on the bed and then her hand on Frank's face to turn his head toward her gaze. His eyes fall gently in hers, before he notices the plane. "Oh God, I'm sorry, Laura. I needed to keep it. To keep him close and not have it remind you...,"

"Shhh, it's okay, Frank. I'm not mad that you needed to keep a piece of him to yourself. I'm not mad. Continue with what you were saying," Laura reassures him.

He thanks her from deep within the trenches of where his eyes pull his spirit into his stare. "The things I told to the police were true. The turmoil twisting in my guts was too much. I needed to accept that he was dead and not coming back, Laura. Our sweet little boy. He's gone." Frank sobs. Laura remains still, combating her own sorrow.

"I want to live again, Laura," he explains, "and I want you to do the same." He places his hand over the one she holds to his cheek. "But, to do that, you need to accept. In my acceptance of what I couldn't change about Billy's short life, I realized there was so much more I refused to deal with through my own. It's time to accept all that we can't erase or change, Laura."

Laura lowers her hand, his still holding on. His fingers resemble prolonged frostbite. "I can bleed black forever, but none of it will continue to keep me from living anymore," Frank continues, "There was nothing I should have ever held against you. It happened, as the unexplainable tends to do...it just happened to us. What I want, and what I hope, is that you can find a way to forgive yourself, because you didn't do anything wrong, Laura. You were an amazing mother to an amazing son. It was an accident."

Laura's eyes hold like a dam about to break. She retracts her hand from his.

"I don't blame you for going back to that place. I only want us to find some sort of individual happiness again," Frank says.

Laura finally responds, her words stained with hopelessness. "Happiness is too far away for me, Frank."

The door to the room opens and a nurse walks in. "Excuse me, sorry to bother, but you are stretching the limit of visiting hours. We're gonna have to ask you to leave now."

Laura pulls the straps of her handbag over her arm. "I'll be back tomorrow," she tells Frank, placing her hand on his shoulder, "And even though I can't be, I want you to be...happy."

Frank grins, then his focus meanders to the window where his father lingers. Laura stares at the window, and to the nurse's bewilderment, sticks her middle finger up in the direction of it and says, "Fuck you."

Laura apologizes to the nurse and leaves. The baffled nurse asks Frank, "Sir, lights on or off?".

He looks at the faint outline of his father in the glass, under the glare of the overhead lights. "Off."

She flips the light off, bringing Sr. into clearer view. His wretched eyes dig like shovels. Some of the black lines on Frank's face grow upward as he stares back. "Yeah, fuck you," Frank yelps. He rolls over in bed with his back to his father, leaving the monster to scream and punch in silence behind the glass.

Of Course, the Beans

Fall 2020

A few strands of moonlight spill through the windows of Frank Nagan's office, illuminating the dark room in a soft, white glow. Some shelves are bare. Others are filled with tchotchkes, books, and certificates. What little furniture exists is surrounded by a variety of moving boxes. The doorknob turns and the door opens, bringing in the light from the hallway. A hand flicks the light switch on, better revealing the clutter. The desk is small with clear blemishes of wear and tear. An accompanying chair's arm rests are wrapped with duct tape at the ends. On top of the desk sits a charcuterie board full of meats and cheeses. Next to it, a bottle of champagne and two glasses. A sheet hangs over a section of the wall farthest from the doorway.

"Almost there," Laura says, as she leads a blindfolded Frank into the center of the room.

"Can I look?"

She pushes an empty box out of the way. "Patience, babe."

"You've made me wait long enough."

"One sec," Laura whispers. She sits him down in a cushy, leather chair that faces the sheet on the wall. Frank runs his hands across the smooth leather of the armchair. "I don't even want to know the cost." He laughs.

"Okay, ready," Laura says in Frank's ear.

She removes his blindfold. Frank adjusts his eyes and looks around the room in awe. "Babe, the walls look amazing! You've outdone yourself." Then, he looks at his new leather chair. "And this, I mean, it's perfect!"

"Next, we get you a boss-ass desk to go with it. You're going to look fucking hot," she exclaims. Laura grabs the champagne and glasses from the desk. Frank continues to study the room, his jaw on the floor. "Do you like it?" She smirks and hands the champagne bottle to Frank. He goes to uncork it and Laura stops him. "Wait, there's one more thing!"

Frank lowers the champagne bottle to his lap. "Oh, you mean that mysterious sheet? Thought it might have just been a very flat ghost."

Laura rolls her eyes at the joke.

"What, I thought you married me for my sense of humor?" he quips.

"Think again, hot shot."

Laura walks over to the sheet. "You worked so hard to get here, babe. I'm so proud of you. I know what this all means to you and you're going to be so successful. I wanted to do something special for you. I hope you like it."

Laura yanks the sheet away to reveal a hand-painted mural of the Nagan Lawn & Land logo. It consists of three bright, green trees within a white circle that's affixed against a red backdrop. The text is big and bold. Frank sits surprised and eases his way out of his seat with the champagne bottle in his hand. "Like it? I fucking love it, babe!" He rejoices, pulling her in and planting a kiss on her lips.

Laura grabs the wrist of the hand holding the bottle and raises it. "Now, you may do the honors, Mr. Nagan."

Frank stares at the painting, moving closer to it to study the minute detailing Laura put into it. He places the bottle down on a moving box and heads to the opposite side of the room.

"Did I miss something?" Laura asks. She steps closer to the mural.

"You know, it's a funny thing," Frank says, scouring through some of the boxes on the floor. "The minute I signed the leasing agreement, I knew I had to have you on my wall." He spots the box he's looking for and opens it. Reaching in, he removes a flat rectangle wrapped in newspaper. He removes the paper, revealing one of Laura's paintings. An abstract of three figures.

"No, not the beans one, Frank," Laura gasps.

He walks to the wall adjacent to the mural and sizes the painting against it. "Of course, the beans one," he says, rummaging through a small toolbox on the ground for a hammer, nail, and level. With the level set horizontally, he marks a spot with the tip of the nail. A few smacks with the hammer and the nail is set, to which he drapes the taut wire of the painting over it. He steps back to take in the entire wall that encompasses the painting and the mural. "Perfect."

Laura pops the champagne from behind, startling him. "Sorry! You were taking too long!" she says.

The champagne overflows. To keep from staining the rug Laura drinks directly from the bottle, quickly passing it to Frank when her mouth is full. He takes a big gulp of bubbly and sets the bottle down.

"I love you," he confesses.

"I love you!" Laura smiles and Frank leans in to kiss her.

She motions toward the food on the desk. "I got all your

favorites. You hungry?"

"I've gotta be honest, babe. I'd much rather fuck you on the new chair than eat."

"I was hoping you'd say that."

Laura turns him down into the chair to straddle him. She places her lips on his, and they share a passionate kiss. Laura peels her mouth away and looks Frank in the eyes. Her face is splashed in moonlight. "But, after, we are totally going to eat, right? I got an amazing Gruyère," Laura says, half-jokingly.

Frank gleefully attacks her in the chair, biting at her neck. "I've got my Gruyère right here!"

Lover Alone

Spring 2013

*E*llis is sound asleep, naked on the ground below the apple tree within JoJo. Vibrant stretches of color breathe around him, ornate and detailed, while also maintaining soft and smokey edges. The needle of his record player has fallen off the side of the vinyl cued up on the turntable: *The Downward Spiral* by Nine Inch Nails. Bullet rests nearby, casually looking about to pass the time. Something stirs through the window to the outside world. Bullet nudges Ellis awake with his head against his face. "What is it?"

The deer walks towards the bark of the tree, staring into the real world. Ellis sits up and rubs the tired from his eyes, his skin glowing under a green sunshine. He joins his companion, both looking through the doorway. A man idles directly outside JoJo. Confident that the man cannot see him inside the tree, Ellis moves closer to get a better look at him.

He is an older gentleman, his brown skin glistening bright under the outside sunshine. What's left of the hair on his head and the beard on his face is starch white. He is dressed in beige slacks and a maroon windbreaker. The wrinkles at the corner of his eyes droop from time. He looks forward into the void he cannot see, with Ellis unknowingly inches from his face.

The man's hand raises and gently caresses the *C.A. & J.L.* etched into the bark. His eyes close and he speaks words Ellis cannot hear. When he opens them again, tears sit on the edges of his eyes. The man lowers his hand and finds a comfortable spot to sit in the grass before the tree. He removes a small mp3 player from his pocket and puts the headphones in his ear. Hours pass and he listens to music alone, occasionally standing up to sway back and forth, pretending to dance with someone who isn't there.

Ellis goes to his pile of records and digs through them until he finds the one he wants. He unsheathes it and places it on the player. *The Letter/Neon Rainbow* by The Box Tops plays and Ellis moves in rhythm around JoJo trying his best to match the speed and movements of the man. He struts when the man struts. He bumps his hips when the man does. He twists and turns and contorts his face with the same feelings as the man. Both their bodies wildly rejoice in the freedom of the music. Ellis playfully circles around Bullet who sits, disinterested. "C'mon, move your feet, Bullet. Don't be boring." The deer doesn't react.

Ellis dances back toward the doorway. The man slows down and eventually stops, removing the player from his pocket to turn it off. Ellis stops dancing. The man takes one last look at JoJo, before disappearing back into the woods from which he came.

Sedative Settle In

Winter 2031

*L*aura spends the morning watching Frank sleep. His veins are still the same rivers of abyss, yet he breathes peacefully as the hours pass. She casually strokes his forehead, studying the black lines in his face, the rot more defined in the daylight. Laura gets up and closes the blinds to cover Frank from the sun. He begins to twitch and mumble in his sleep. She returns to his side, lowering her ear to his mouth because she can't understand him. His eyes remain closed. The grumbling grows louder. His body, more erratic.

"Frank, you're okay. I'm right here," Laura says.

She tries to shake him out of his nightmare. The damp fire from his skin can be felt through the hospital gown. His eyes burst open; pupils black as night. He yells, "Get the belt. Get the belt. Get the belt," and grabs Laura's arm hard. A deep, unrecognizable chill swirling in the nothingness of his eyes bores into her. "Get the belt!

Get the belt!"

"Frank, I'm here. Listen to my words."

She holds his face to calm him. It doesn't work. He screams the same words louder and louder. Hospital staff barrels in and backs Laura out of the way.

"GET THE BELT! GET THE BELT!"

A nurse draws a syringe and sticks it in Frank's arm. Laura watches her husband slip into unconsciousness. "Is he going to be okay?"

One of the doctors approaches Laura, poised in his body language. "Hello, Mrs. Nagan. I'm Dr. Nant. Your husband is under a lot of duress right now and we are working our hardest on getting to the bottom of this. A remarkable hematologist, Dr. Rolinga, is scheduled to see him today and run a few more tests. It is my advice, for the time being, we quarantine."

"Quarantine? Why? What aren't you telling me?"

"Mrs. Nagan, I understand this isn't what you want to hear, but because we cannot determine your husband's condition, we can't risk the spread of potential contagion," Dr. Nant explains.

***

Laura sits in her car in the hospital parking lot. Billy's toy plane rests on the passenger's seat. She starts the SUV with a press of her thumbprint on the steering wheel. The dashboard, completely touch screen, lights up and a disc jockey on the radio kicks in. "Halfway through the Alamo hour, let's keep the rock rollin'. This is Ricky Alamo and you're listening to KWP, home to all things classic rock. This next track recently celebrated its 35th birthday. 'Guerilla Radio' from a little band called Rage Against the Machine!"

Laura reverses, almost rear ended by a car speeding through the lot. Infuriated, she yells, "You motherfucker!" and takes off in pursuit of the other vehicle, cutting it off at the exit. The man in the car lays on his horn. Laura puts her car in park and gets out, the music blasting from the radio. She walks around the front of her car and up to the man, who has already lowered his window.

"What the fuck, lady?"

Laura is incensed. "What the fuck, me? Are you kidding? You almost clipped me back there, asshole. You could've killed someone. Slow the fuck down!"

"Everyone is fine. So, maybe relax a bit," the man says.

Laura reaches through the window and pulls the man forward by the collar. "Because of shitty, irresponsible, careless people like you, I can't fucking relax." Her fists tighten around his shirt.

"Alright lady, I'm sorry. Now, could you let me go before I have to call the cops?"

Laura looks down to the man's neck as if she's only now realizing her hands are on him. She releases her grip and apologizes. He reverses, then squeezes around her car in the direction of the exit. She gets back in her SUV and closes the door, cranking the volume of the music all the way up to hide the sound of her screams. Her lungs empty every morsel of mourning into the noise.

A Boy and His Plane

November 22, 2031

*T*he Wyland Mall is jam packed with holiday shoppers. Parents tagging children along with them; some pushing strollers with toddlers half asleep. Couples walk hand in hand, lazily looking at the clothes on sale. Below the escalator, kids impatiently wait for their turn on Santa's lap. Certain stores have lines out the front, wrapping past the entrances of others. A little away from the hustle and bustle of the mall, Laura and Billy sit at the food court, finishing their lunch, with a dozen shopping bags at their feet. Billy's plane sits beside his tray. He dips a chicken nugget into a container of barbecue sauce and watches the small Ferris Wheel in the center of the food court spin while he chews. Laura stays on her cell phone, texting and periodically checks that Billy is eating his food.

"Mommy, can we do the Ferris Wheel before we go?"

Without looking up from her phone, Laura says, "Sorry, bubba, we don't have time today. We need to meet daddy after work so we can go pick out our Christmas tree, remember?"

"Oh, right! We gotta get a real big one this year," Billy suggests.

"We got a real big one last year as well."

"We need to get a bigger one, with...with...," Billy stutters, trying to find the right words and says, "With a million branches of glitter and bells. We need them all, mommy."

Laura slips her phone into her pocket and looks up. "Is that right?" She cleans the sauce from the corners of Billy's lips. "Be sure to let daddy know."

Billy finishes the last nugget from his tray.

"Go, toss out your trash, bubs. We need to get going," Laura says.

He gulps the last of the juice he had and slinks off his chair to his feet. He carefully brings his tray to the nearest garbage and places it onto a flat, robotic arm that pulls it into a slot at the top of the pail and empties it. He hesitates to return to watch the Ferris Wheel a bit longer. It stops spinning and a mother and daughter at the top yell with excitement. Billy giggles to himself.

Laura gathers as many bags in her hands as possible, and swings her handbag over her shoulder, leaving the lightest ones for Billy to carry. "Bubs, there you go. Pick those up for mommy, will ya?"

He picks them up and the two of them leave the food court. On their way down the escalator, Laura looks at the bags in her hand and disappointment flushes across her face. "Ugh, I forgot to get wrapping paper."

"Mommy, over there." Billy points his little finger in the direction of the Dollar Tree. A box filled with rolls of wrapping paper is positioned near the entrance of the store.

The Dollar Tree is well lit up for Christmas. People scattered between the rows, some checking the integrity of items and placing them back on the shelves. Laura drops all the bags by the front counter to give her hands a rest. The wrapping paper display is within her eye line.

"Go, grab mom three rolls. Any will do, bubs."

Billy retrieves the wrapping paper and brings them back. The two of them wait in line for longer than Laura would like to.

Billy looks into every bag in Laura's hands. "Where is my plane?"

"It's in one of these bags. Don't you worry!"

They finally reach the cashier. Laura waves her phone over the debit machine to pay.

Hustling now, the two of them move about the crowd, squeezing past every hole between people they can fit through. "We've got to pick up the pace, bubs." Laura's voice hastens along with her feet. Billy keeps up, both bobbing and weaving until they hit the parking garage.

At her SUV, Laura puts the bags down by the trunk. Billy does the same, putting his bags on the ground by the rear tire. Laura presses her thumb to the sun emblem on the trunk hatch. It raises on its own. "Get in, bubs."

Billy pulls on the handle of the backdoor, but it's still locked. He spots his plane on top of some items in one of the bags and takes it out. Frazzled, Laura piles the bags into the trunk as fast as she can. Between their vehicle and the one parked next to it, Billy zips his plane around with his hand to pretend it's flying, mimicking engine and propeller noises with his mouth.

"All done," Laura says. She starts lowering the trunk hatch, believing she's put all the bags away, and sees the three Billy left by the tire. She lets the trunk open again and goes around to get the stragglers. Billy moves out of her way, aimlessly backing himself into the driving lane of the garage. Laura throws the bags into the back of the SUV and slams the trunk closed. Billy's flying noises alert her to his whereabouts. "C'mon, bubs."

Laura turns around just in time to catch the fender of a screeching car smack against Billy's head. The impact sends his body to the pavement and the toy plane through the air onto another parked car. In complete shock, she stumbles to his body and falls to the ground. It's difficult for her to see through the tint on the windshield of the car that hit him. She shakes more violently as reality sets in. Bystanders begin to gather as she scoops his limp body into her arms, his eyes slowly blinking and eventually still.

"Someone call 9-1-1!"

Avoid the Unavoidable

Winter 2031

*L*aura steps into the void. Billy appears from the apple tree and runs up to her, hugging her waist. Her fingers dishevel his hair. Then, she bends down and gives him his plane. He grabs it, ecstatic to have it back. Racing around, he flies it through the air without another care in the world.

"How's Frank?" Ellis approaches from behind.

"I don't really want to talk about it right now." Laura sweeps her eyes across the void. "Tell me more about you instead. How are you?"

"Don't get asked that very often," Ellis admits.

"Well, you just did. So, out with it."

"I miss Marie. I miss her food, her laugh, the freedom her kindness gave me. I miss her overflowing bookshelves that smelled like a time before me. She taught me how to lose all the bad things in the pages. How to shake your hips and let music remind you that you're alive," Ellis vomits out, making his way to the record player. He puts on a Miles Davis album and returns to Laura. "She was a saint when I needed one and every time since, that I get spit back out, has never been the same. It's never been happy. I either got used or used others for my own survival. With her, life out there felt like something worth enjoying. But all good things get ripped apart eventually."

"All things must pass," Laura says.

"George Harrison. My favorite Beatle," Ellis says, smirking.

"Do you think, deep down, you like being here?" Laura asks.

"I don't like it, but I don't always mind that it isn't out there."

"I get that, I do," Laura says, "Sometimes I feel so distant from any understanding of why we are put on this rock. To hope for the best, but prepare to inevitably endure the worst? It's fucked up. Even before Billy, most days I wanted to run and hide in the farthest corner of my house and pretend nothing exists outside my front door."

Billy and Bullet play in the distance. Ellis's sight hangs on them. "The thing that really boggles my mind about the day I got stuck here," Ellis says, his sight hanging on the deer and the boy in the distance, "is I thought I was doing the right thing. We needed food. I was following orders. Why punish a kid for that?"

"Is something right or is it just all we know…I ask myself that all the time. We justify our existence based on surrounding circumstances, with little knowledge of how this all works. Of how the unseen and unknown carries on around us. I don't know that one ever truly grasps the secrets of nature," Laura says.

"And that is exactly why it became easier to accept being here. My mind could only do so much searching for answers it'll never find. Sanity, some shard of peace, it came with acceptance," Ellis says.

Laura focuses on Billy teasing Bullet with the plane.

"You know, I'm allergic to dander," she admits.

Ellis turns his attention to her.

"He wanted a dog, but we could never get one because of me. It breaks my heart when I think of it now. We should've gotten him the fucking dog," Laura bemoans.

"Bullet's no dog, but he'll do," Ellis says, outlining them in red from a distance with his finger. "He seems to love that toy."

"He became obsessed with planes because of his dad. Frank would build models in some of his spare time. Billy became transfixed. One birthday, we got him a bunch of toy planes. That one was his favorite. It never left his side." The smile on her face fades against the bitterness of her reality. "He was like Frank; in the way he knew what he wanted and would obsess until achieving it. Even as a boy, he shared the same determination in his eyes as Frank did. There was never a doubt in my mind he wouldn't grow up to become a pilot or astronaut." She's crushed with what can never be. Her attention recedes within. She trails off.

"Want to talk about it?" Ellis asks.

She sidesteps the question. "How about we get you some new clothes? Or, I should say new, old clothes. I have bags of Frank's old shit that I haven't gotten around to dropping at Goodwill. You can have them."

"I can?"

"Yeah. You could do with an update," she says, a teasing grin on her face.

Go from God

Spring 1944

*T*he war report plays over the radio at a low volume. Crushed beer cans line the countertop in the kitchen. Breadcrumbs mill around a sink full of dirty dishes. Thick layers of dust settle atop the shelves on the wall. A window above the sink is closed, as are the blinds, to keep out the afternoon light.

Michael Foster sits at the kitchen table cleaning the barrel of his rifle. The scruff on his face is uneven. His bushy hair is flattened from grease and sweat. Periodically, he stops using the barrel brush to sip from a freshly opened beer.

In the living room, Ellis sits on the floor in front of the empty fireplace with letter blocks. He uses them to spell out three- and four-letter words like "cat" and "blue". The room is drab. Furniture is tired with flattened cushions. Mildew stains collect in various corners, accompanied by cobwebs. He grows bored with his blocks and watches his father from where he sits.

Michael can sense the weight of the boy's eyes. "What is it?"

Ellis averts and tilts his head to the floor.

Michael places the rifle down on the table and waves the boy over. His words slur. "You're going to have to learn this one day or another."

Ellis walks into the kitchen and stands at the edge of the table, his eyeline just breaching the surface. Michael turns the barrel away from him.

"Never stand in front of the barrel!"

Ellis is startled. Michael points to the chair opposite him. "Sit across from me, right there."

Michael continues cleaning the barrel, throwing glances at Ellis struggling to pull himself up into the chair. On the table before him is a box of bullets. Michael notices the boy's focus on the box and motions for him to open it. Ellis slides the box to the edge of the table and carefully lifts the top.

"Go ahead," Michael says.

Ellis removes one of the bullets and analyzes it. The bronze chunk of metal is almost bigger than his hand. He turns the tip toward himself and squints to focus one eye on its narrow point.

"That, right there, is power," Michael tells him. He reaches across the table and snatches the bullet from the boy. He holds the bullet up in one hand and the gun in his other. "Together, these are the keys to survival, you understand that?"

Ellis doesn't respond. His attention oscillates between the gun and the bullet.

"Of course, you don't. You don't understand anything yet. You don't know what it's like out there, in the real world. You don't know what survival is because I have to do everything for you." Michael's words get swallowed with his beer. He places the gun down on the table in front of him when a knock at the door commands their attention.

Michael gulps down the rest of his beer, a few drops of it disappear in his beard. "Answer it. Go, greet the real world, son."

Ellis jumps off the chair, scuttles to the front door, and opens it. Outside stands a priest with two teenage boys holding pamphlets.

"Hello, son! Are your parents home?" The priest asks.

Ellis looks back to his father in the kitchen. The priest follows suit and makes eye contact with Michael. "Hello, Sir. My name is Father Middleton. Might I borrow your ear for a few minutes?" The priest's bright smile fills the house.

Michael stands and, to the discomfort of the three guests, swings the rifle over his shoulder. He combs his messy hair with his fingers as he moves towards the door to greet the trio. One of the boys holds out a pamphlet for a fundraiser. Michael takes it, sweeping his eyes through it for a couple of seconds. "Not interested. Don't have anything to spare," Michael says. He hands the pamphlet back to the boy.

The priest steps between the two boys to face Michael, keeping with niceties. "Sir, we mean no harm and only come to spread the word of the Lord and hope our neighbors and their neighbors can find it in their hearts to give good tidings. St. Sebastian's is in need of some repairs."

Michael removes the gun from his shoulder and rests the butt of it on the floor, holding onto the barrel. The two boys behind the priest exchange scared looks.

"What does this have to do with me?" Michael questions. His patience is thinning.

The priest's nerves are a bit rattled. "Well, I was going through Father Willan's address book and one Michael & Joanne Foster were listed at this address. Seems it's been some time since we've seen you at mass, so I thought I'd stop by and..."

"Ask my dead wife and I for money?" Michael interrupts. His ice-cold stare slices through the young priest.

Father Middleton and the boys are stunned. Ellis backs away from the door as his father gets closer to the priest, who is stumbling through his words. "Mr. Foster, on behalf of the congregation, I apologize. I didn't mean to offend or speak out of place."

Michael interjects once more, moving closer to the priest with every word. "Take your ugly pamphlets. Take your absent God. And take your useless prayers from my doorstep before I use this thing." He raises the rifle with both hands.

"Boys, let us leave Mr. Foster be and carry on elsewhere," cautions Father Middleton. He grabs both the boys by their shirts and leads them back down the front walkway. Michael watches them leave, then slams the door shut behind them, locking it. He rests the gun against the wall beside the door and turns back toward the kitchen.

Ellis, standing in the middle of the living room, stares up at the urn above the fireplace. "What was mommy like?"

Michael takes pause, then proceeds to walk by Ellis without answering. He lumbers into the kitchen, opens the refrigerator, and grabs a new beer.

Different Sized Holes

Winter 2031

*A*s they pull into the driveway, Ellis is struck by the Nagan's two-story ranch.

"Beautiful house, Laura."

"Thanks. We both fell in love with it the moment we saw it, but it's not so much a home anymore. Just a place where I cry, mostly." She laughs to herself.

Laura gives him a quick tour downstairs. Ellis soaks up the long-arched windows and wooden floors and high-end gadgets. He admires the photos of a once-happy Nagan family on various walls. Everything in the house looked in its place, as though it had no idea of the train wreck its occupants were going through.

Upstairs, she shows him her art studio. It's a small room tucked at the end of the hallway past the staircase. Her artwork hangs from every wall. Abstracts of people and figures, all seemingly content, but not without twinges of sadness. Honest depictions of humanity in a sea of the absurd. Ellis is lost in them. Laura watches him. "What are you thinking about?"

Without looking away from the wall, he remarks, "How we are all stuck in different sized holes, trying to find beauty amongst the shadows glued to us."

Laura is caught off guard by the response, unable to conjure words.

"Do you ever wish to pick it up again?" he asks.

Laura scans her own work, lets out a pessimistic sigh and concedes. "Maybe, one day."

She stops before a painting which resembles Frank. "Have you ever seen anything from that place show itself outside?" she asks. Ellis relinquishes focus from her artwork. "What do you mean?"

"It's Frank. And...and his father. He sees him everywhere now. And he's sick. Not like how you described you get, but with this black stuff under his skin. The hospital may never let him go because they're testing him for something that isn't even of this world."

Ellis straightens and takes a step closer, listening without interruption.

"Poor Frank, he has always worried he'd become just like his dad," Laura confesses, "He's worked so hard to get through all those feelings, and now that fucker is back. It's unfair. That man was awful. Really messed Frank up...I didn't cry when he died."

"Nothing has ever escaped that place before," Ellis says, "It's always been pretty routine. It opens at the beginning of the winter when it is most depleted and hungry, usually somewhere around 15-20 years from when I last fed it. It gives me until spring starts to find another victim. It closes once I do. Everything that appears for people is tied to their grief and, if there's one thing I've learned all these years, grief comes in all shapes and sizes. It's hard to say if that's normal or not, because I don't think I'll ever fully get it. For the longest time

I'd associate it with some kind of Heaven, but if something that ugly was waiting to escape, maybe it's just, like, some kind of mirror to our humanity, our individual heartache."

"There's got to be something we can do," Laura insists.

Ellis paces around in thought. "Maybe when the cycle ends and JoJo closes back up, Frank's father's connection will be severed. We just need to keep Frank safe until then," Ellis suggests.

"How do we watch over him if he's quarantined?"

"We bust him out," Ellis opines with confidence.

Laura half-jokingly agrees. "Yeah, sure, we can sneak him right out of the hospital."

"Okay," Ellis responds, all in on the idea, "tonight, we get him out and make this right. I'll figure it out."

Laura ponders the thought. "Fuck it. Let's do it."

Transference

Winter 2031

*B*illy skips about an open field of grass splashed in multicolored luminescence, flying his plane in circles. His little body flutters and the pigmentation reverberates across his skin. Bullet watches from a few feet away, curled atop a flat rock that sticks out slightly above the grass, the pink sun shining down on him. There is contentment in their silence. This bliss, however, is short lived.

The monster, Frank Sr., slimes up from the roots of the apple tree; his blackened, half-body casts the same shadow. It is a wild, tentacle-like blob that renders the rays of the sun useless, snapping both Billy and Bullet's attention from their field of dreams. Sr. lurches toward them, sucking the color and life from each blade of grass he touches. A trail of tar settles in his wake.

Billy is frozen, locked onto the unnatural abscess closing in on him. Bullet watches the boy, petrified, and takes initiative, approaching the monster. Sr. shifts his attention to the deer and swings a tentacle in Bullet's direction, causing the frightened animal to cower.

Imposing over his grandson now, Sr. bends to one knee. The deep and hollow nothingness of his pupils idle before the boy. The monster raises its hand and passes it over the toy plane, illuminating a handprint on its wing. The print is much too large to be Billy's. The boy observes it, holding his little hand just above the wing to compare sizes. Sr.'s hand now hovers over Billy's, the blackened tar dripping from his fingers. Billy pulls his hand away before it lands on him. He holds the plane out to the monster, offering it up. Sr. wraps his hand around the fingerprints. In the length of a breath, he and the plane vanish from the void.

Hand Me Downs

Winter 2031

*L*aura and Ellis exit the studio. He stops to investigate a room at the end of the hallway, its door ajar. The walls appear blue, and the edge of a bed juts out into his line of sight. A poster of an astronaut with his thumb up faces Ellis from the wall in the open doorway. Model planes and toys line the shelves above and below it. A heavy silence briefly sucks the air from where they stand. Laura closes the door. "I've been meaning to clean it out, but-"

"You don't have to explain," Ellis says.

Laura is grateful. She opens the door to her room and invites Ellis in. He stops in the doorway, hesitant to enter the bedroom. "Can't try them on out there," she says, flopping two bags from the closet onto her bed.

Ellis enters, an awkward weight in his steps. The bedroom is ultra-modern. Three of the four walls are light gray, occupied by several larger paintings. A bold, red accent wall displays a massive flat screen television bookended by speakers; all built flush into the wall. Below the television is a horizontal shelving unit with family photos lined across the top of it. On the opposite side of the room is a king-sized bed covered in a blanket that matches the accent wall. Hanging above the bed, nearly the entire size of the ceiling, is a detailed and colorful woven tapestry of the universe. The sun, the moon, the planets, and the stars, all existing together. Laura starts pulling shirts from the bags and holds them to Ellis's body, sizing with her eyes. She makes two separate piles.

"Why are you making two piles?"

"One for what I think will fit you and one for what won't," she says, not quite paying attention.

They go through the same process with pants. Ellis can't help but stare at her fingers, which brush his waistline as she holds a pair of black jeans against him. Laura looks up and catches him entranced by her contact. She pulls back and drops the pants in the "try on" pile.

"You can use the master bathroom to see what fits."

He grabs the clothes from the pile and asks, "Would it be okay to take a shower?"

Predator/Prey

───────── 🍎 ─────────

Winter 2031

*T*he door to Frank's hospital room is cracked open. The hallway bustle of an adjoining nurse station spills in. A steady beep from the heart monitor attaches itself to the stale hum of the room. Frank's unconscious breaths fog the inside of a plastic quarantine cover fitted to the bed. Every vein beneath his skin has blackened. His body is drenched with sweat, the sheets dark with moisture. The blinds are closed to block out the sun, allowing only slivers of light to seep in at their edges.

Frank's eyes begin to roll under his closed eyelids. His body twitches. The black veins in the palm of his right hand swell and wriggle like worms under his skin. They burst and the poison fills in Frank's handprint completely, all the way up to the tips of his fingers.

Within the darkened cover of the window closest to his bed, Sr. appears from the depths of nothing. His head twists and contorts as he raises the plane into sight, the handprint on the wing glowing. The monster presses his hand to it and Frank's hand darkens further. Sr., then, places his open palm against the windowpane. A hole, like that of the doorway into the void, opens. Into the room, the monster steps with Billy's plane in his hand. He slithers his way up to the side of the bed, his tentacle shadow thrashing on the wall behind him.

The poison drips from the shifting blacks and grays of his form, collecting on the floor like an oil spill. He leans as close to the plastic cover as possible. His dead, black eyes glint with the reflection of Frank's EKG lines. He watches his prey with a cold death in his eyes - vacuums looking for a soul to steal. And Frank, in the arms of his dreams, remains an injured rodent unaware of a circling vulture.

Friendly Little Reminders

Fall 2022

A plane full of passengers makes a descent toward its destination. Frank sits in a window seat, while Laura sleeps against his shoulder. His foot taps nervously against the floor as he watches the ground get closer through the window. Laura is startled awake when the wheels touch the tarmac. The plane rattles down the airstrip to a near stop and turns toward the airport to dock.

"Over under on your brother being on time?" Laura asks.

Frank rolls his eyes.

The two of them collect their luggage from the baggage claim and stand on the sidewalk of the pick-up lane. Laura uses her luggage as a seat. The sun hangs low in the sky over the terminal. Passengers come and go around them.

A pickup truck lays on its horn as it pulls over in front of them. The driver waves emphatically through the windshield. Laura smiles and waves back. Frank merely grins and nods in response.

The man gets out and comes around the truck to greet them. He's a couple of years younger than Frank, dressed in dirty blue jeans and boots, with a flannel shirt half-buttoned over a black t-shirt. A sweat stained baseball cap sits on his head. Long brown hair pours out from its sides. His face is covered in scruff. "My God, haven't seen you two in forever. Laura! Looking top-shelf as usual," the man says. He goes in for a hug. Laura reciprocates.

"Jamie, still a charmer, I see," she says.

Frank steps forward as the two of them release from the hug. Jamie puts his hands on his waist and looks Frank over from top to bottom. Frank wears brown shoes, fit slacks, and a neat, collared shirt under a slim cut sport coat.

"Looking sharp, Frankie."

"You're late," Frank says.

Jamie takes his cap off and curls the brim nervously. "Sorry about that. Lot goin' on around here, Frank. Work. Wife. Pop."

Frank stiffens at the mention of their father.

"Pay him no mind. He's just a grump from the flight," Laura says.

"We've gotta keep it moving, people," an airport employee shouts at them.

Jamie hurries to the back of his truck and lowers the cab door. Frank carries their luggage over and loads it into the truck bed, under the vinyl cover.

"I was hoping to have Lil's car, but she had a million errands to run today," Jamie says. He opens the passenger side door and pulls a lever to swing the seat forward. Behind it is a small cabin with a bench seat. "Will have to do for now, Laura. Sorry."

"It's fine. Frank and I are happy you could come get us. Seriously, it's fine." Laura climbs into the back and pulls the front seat toward her so Frank can get in.

202

Jamie runs around the front of the truck and gets in.

"We aren't more than thirty minutes from here. Easy ride. I think Lil is doing a pot roast tonight," he says.

"How far is the hospital?" Frank asks.

***

Jamie enters the room first, with Frank and Laura behind him. There is only one bed in the center of the room. A frail, nearly comatose Frank Sr. lies under the sheets with tubes coming out of his nose and from between his legs. Even more lines feed out from his arms to monitors and the I.V. drip.

Jamie leans over the bed railing, close to his father's ear. "Hey, Pop. You've got some visitors."

Sr.'s eyelids flutter but don't fully open.

Frank steps further into the room, around to the other side of his father. Laura stands at the foot of the bed.

"He's looking good considering, don't you think, Frankie?" Jamie asks.

Frank stares down at his father, quietly.

"I guess you wouldn't have much to compare it to though. Been what, three years?"

"Four," Frank says, with little emotion.

Jamie looks up from his father to Frank. The two of them trade stiff, resentful looks.

"I'll leave you two to it," Jamie says to Frank. Then, louder, into his father's ear, while rubbing the sick man's shoulder, he says, "I'll be back tomorrow. Love ya, Pop."

"I'll join you," Laura says. She gives Frank a kiss on the cheek. "I'm right outside if you need me."

Jamie holds the door for Laura and then closes it behind himself, leaving Frank alone with their father. Frank pulls a chair from the wall at the foot of the bed and brings it to where he was standing. He unbuttons his coat and takes a seat. Sr.'s head faces

Frank's direction. His eyes are still closed, his breath long and slow. Frank clears his throat.

"I don't know if you can actually hear me, but it's Frankie."

Sr.'s eyes roll under his eyelids at the sound of Frank's voice.

"I've thought long and hard about what to say here and I want you to know that I'm not here for you. I'm here for Jamie. Because, for some strange reason, he sees you as someone worth grieving. You only get me today and at your funeral, understand?"

His father's head shifts slightly. The old man's fingers tremble amongst the top of the sheets.

"My whole life, there's been this shadow looming. It sounds just like you. Terrorizes just like you. I still wear the scars on my body, you know that? Friendly little reminders."

Frank takes a pause, running his hands through his hair. He sucks back the emotions trickling into his eyes. "Here I am, still able to be sad for you. It's insane. How could someone do that to their son? Be so cruel. I never understood it. Not sure I ever will. And now, what? I'm supposed to hold your hand while you're afraid and dying?" Frank laughs to himself. His father's eyelids lift a hair, but the feeble man has a tough time keeping them open.

"Despite everything you did. All that ugliness. I'm here to tell you I'm successful, madly in love, and will never treat my children the way you treated me. You never kept me down. I became everything you weren't able to. Now, you open your eyes again. You hear me, Pop? Open them."

Frank stands up. Sr. struggles to adjust his head but faces upwards and opens his eyes as wide as possible. "I will never forget, but to be free of you, this is what I have to do," Frank says, leaning down with his hands on the bed railing, inches from his father's face, "The demons, they're of my own making, and have been for years. I never thought this would be possible to do...but...I forgive you, Pop."

Sr. fights to open his mouth and raise his hand. Frank leans closer. His father's lips shake and give up, unable to muster any words. Instead, his pockmarked hand locates Frank's along the railing and grabs hold. The two of them locked in each other's glare, Sr.'s eyes fill with contempt. He pushes Frank's hand from the railing.

Frank takes a deep breath and buttons his coat. "Enjoy the rest of your life," he says, before exiting. The door gradually closes behind him. Sr. is alone.

The Heist

Winter 2031

The sun is setting behind the hospital when they arrive. Warm, fuchsia streaks stretch across the sky as if Ellis painted them with his own hands.

The receptionist sits at her desk, her skin pale and hair in a neat ponytail. Laura walks past her towards the elevators.

"Excuse me, ma'am," the receptionist calls out.

Laura plays dumb. "Yes?"

"You have to sign in," the receptionist says, politely.

Laura walks back to the desk and signs in. "Sorry. I'm here to visit Room 409. Nagan is the name."

The receptionist types the name in. Her disposition shifts. "Ma'am, I am going to have to ask you to take a seat. I will have Dr. Rolinga down to see you."

"I can't go up and see my own husband?"

"Ma'am, please, have a seat. The doctor will be down to speak with you."

Laura raises her voice, shoving things on the reception desk. "My husband is in there and you're telling me-"

"Calm down, ma'am, or I'm gonna have to call security."

The security guard is already on his way over. Ellis waits for him to pass. Then, he walks behind the guard, past the reception desk. He pushes the elevator button and stands nervously, watching the numbers in the display above the elevator descend.

"Sir," he hears from behind. Ellis pays no mind and steps closer to the elevator. Before it has a chance to reach the lobby, another security guard steps in front of Ellis.

"Sir, the receptionist needs you to sign in."

Ellis is walked to the front desk. Laura and he exchange looks, disappointed that their plan didn't work.

"He's with me. Leave him be," Laura admits.

The receptionist points at two seats for them to wait.

"I'm sorry, Laura."

"It wasn't your fault," she says, her tone flat.

"It worked wonderfully in a book I once read," Ellis says.

Laura shifts in her seat to face him.

"They got past the guard and up to the room and helped the prisoner escape."

"A story from a book?" Laura snaps. She is frustrated and embarrassed. "This is real life, Ellis, not some fairytale bullshit."

"I'm sorry. I really am, Laura," Ellis pleads.

Laura doesn't respond. The two of them sit in silence. Several tense minutes pass before Dr. Rolinga joins them in the lobby. She's a short, brown-skinned woman, with her hair tied tightly into a bun on her head, her white coat covering a brown blouse and matching trousers.

"Can I see my husband?"

"I'm afraid that isn't possible at the moment," Dr. Rolinga says, avoidance in her voice, "because it seems he has gone missing. A nurse reported it about two hours ago."

"Two fucking hours?! Were you going to call me?!"

"We are deeply sorry about the miscommunication, Mrs. Nagan. But we have already involved the authorities. It is my understanding he may be suicidal," Dr. Rolinga recounts.

"He isn't. That's a crazy thing to say. Plus, Frank could barely walk. How could he get up and leave?"

"I understand this is an emotional time for your family...,"

"You couldn't possibly understand. I want to search the hospital myself."

Dr. Rolinga offers to accompany her to his room to answer some of the questions the on-site law enforcement may have for her. Ellis stands to walk along with Laura.

"Only direct relatives, Sir," Dr. Rolinga asserts. Ellis doesn't push back and offers to remain in the lobby.

***

Black stains, resembling footprints, grab Laura's attention upon entering the room. Her concentration is broken by Deputy Mattison. "Mrs. Nagan, we are doing all we can to locate Frank."

Laura thanks him and spots Billy's plane sitting in the middle of the empty bed. Deputy Parsons continues with some by-the-numbers questions to establish a possible motive for Frank to up and leave, but Laura mostly tunes her out. Dr. Rolinga stands behind Laura at the door, chiming in between the deputies' questions, attempting to explain that whatever her husband has may have affected his cognitive abilities.

Laura continues to the bed, ignoring the majority of what they have to say; her focus on nothing but the plane. She picks it up against the wishes of everyone in the room. Laura looks up to make eye contact with Deputy Parsons, who now demands she place it down and answer the questions. Over Deputy Parson's shoulder, Laura catches a glimpse of a body hurtling past the window.

Good News for Once

Fall 2024

*T*he leaves on the trees throughout town have all changed. Red, orange, yellow, all of them in the final stages of beauty before death. "Money money money mon-EY...MON-EY," Frank sings to himself as he drums on the steering wheel, excited at the sight of leaves starting to fall across people's lawns. He enters the SuperMart lot and parks. He gets out and slams the door shut, still murmuring a few lyrics of the song as he enters the store.

One by one, down the aisles, he collects ingredients for a recipe on his phone - Sticky Chicken and Plum Tray Bake.

Frank brings his cart to the register.

"Leigh, what's been up?" he says.

"Frank! Nothing much. Good to see ya."

Leigh begins ringing up his items, pausing a moment to observe a few of the ingredients Frank's purchasing. "Looks like you're whipping up something good tonight. You spoil that wife of yours. I'd kill for Howard to cook me a meal. The bum."

"How about I bring you a little something one day, Leigh?"

"Don't make a promise you can't keep, Frank."

"I'll bring just enough for you and you only. Howard's out!"

"Serves him right!" she says. The two share a laugh.

Brian Billips, with a bit more hair on his head, waddles over. "Stop flirting, you two."

Leigh smirks at Brian.

"Frank, my man! How goes it?" Brian asks.

The men shake hands and Frank pulls Brian in for a hug.

"Can't complain. Can't complain. You? How are Callie and Jen doing?" Frank inquires.

"Business is good. Family is good. Jen started high school last month. That's a trip, having your kid slap you with the backhand of reality. They just keep growing," Brian bemuses.

Leigh finishes bagging Frank's groceries. Frank inserts his credit card to pay.

"Don't be too hard on yourself. Getting old isn't all that bad," Frank says.

"Easy for you to say," Leigh exclaims.

"Exactly. You're like, what, thirty-six?" Brian says.

"Thirty-FOUR," Frank says.

"Bastard!" Brian shouts. "Well, good seeing you, Frank. Gotta get back to it. You're going to take care of me, right? Couple of weeks it's going to be a slip and slide out there."

"You already know, we've got you covered," Frank replies.

Brian retreats to his office.

Frank collects the bags on the counter. "Later, Leigh!"

"Take it easy, Frank. I'll be waiting impatiently for my dish!"

***

Once home, with arms full of groceries, Frank slams the door shut with his foot.

"Babe?" Frank calls out.

"Upstairs!"

Frank drops the bags on the kitchen counter and makes his way upstairs. He turns the corner at the top of the steps and enters Laura's studio.

"I'm going to make some..." Frank stops in the doorway as Laura stands in anticipation at the center of the room. Her smile widens.

"You okay?" he asks, eyeing around the room.

"More than," she replies.

Laura steps to the side and reveals a painted canvas - the hands of a woman delicately holding her rounded belly.

"Wait..." Frank's mind calculates. His eyes stretch open with realization. "For real?!"

Laura excitedly nods in confirmation. "Mhm, we're going to be parents!"

"Oh my..." Frank scoops Laura up in his arms and gives her a warm hug. Then, he quickly puts her down. "How are you feeling?" he asks.

"Just a little nauseous, but too excited to care."

Frank gently places his hand on her flat stomach. "I love you," he says, pulling her in for a kiss.

Tragic Vacancy

Winter 2031

Down in the lobby, Ellis sits, paging through a hospital pamphlet. He yawns, closes the pamphlet, and stands up. The receptionist and security guard keep an eye on him from their desks. Ellis holds out his hands to signal everything is fine and enters the gift shop.

A petite, older woman with curly, white hair sits on a stool behind the register. A family at the counter purchases a small bouquet of flowers with a heart balloon sticking out of the vase. Ellis walks the aisles full of stuffed animals and "Get-well-soon" gifts, nothing much striking his fancy. On an endcap, below a postcard display, he spots a bin of toy vehicles. Ambulances, police cars, trucks, motorcycles, and, at the very bottom, a fighter jet. He takes it to the counter and buys it.

Back in the lobby, Ellis approaches the receptionist.

"Have they found Frank Nagan yet?"

"Sir, I am not privy to that information at this time. But, even if they did, he is under restricted visiting hours that only apply to immediate family as you've already been told."

Ellis backs off and looks toward the elevators. He is met with a glare from his favorite security guard. He checks his watch.

Outside, he spots the bus stop and heads over as a bus pulls in. A woman getting off notices something in the sky and shrieks. Ellis looks up as a body thuds against the top of the bus and rolls off onto the concrete. Several people gasp and scream. The bus driver gets off the bus to examine what happened and recoils from the sight.

A crowd gathers around the accident. Ellis pushes through to find Frank on the ground, holding his arms, twitching in his own blood. Ellis rushes to his side and grabs his hand as he chokes on the blackened tar dripping from his mouth. Noises of struggle and pain escape Frank's throat in place of words he can no longer speak. Ellis removes the fighter jet from the gift shop bag and holds it out for Frank to see. The horrors of Frank's past wrestle with the soft brown of his pupils; fighting between being his own and the undeniable cauldron of his father's. Ellis places the plane in Frank's hand and closes his fist around it. "You are not him, Frank. He is not you. Don't let him win."

The mangled and contorted Frank breathes deep and overcomes what is left of his monster. His eyes are his own. They stir with questions and worries unable to be spoken, until the dim shroud of emptiness stills them to a tragic vacancy.

Ellis moves out of the way to make room for EMT staff. He looks up to where Frank fell from and locates Laura at a fourth story window, her screams muted by the glass as she beats against it in Deputy Mattison's arms.

I Missed You

Fall 2026

*L*aura is tucked safe against Frank in bed, buried under the warm sheets. His arm is draped over her. They are sound asleep. Their chests bellow in rhythm with each breath they take. All the lights are turned off in the room, except for the glow from a baby monitor screen on Laura's nightstand. In the monitor, Billy wriggles himself awake and his cries fill the room. Frank rolls over onto his back; a soft yawn escapes him. Laura rubs her eyes awake and looks at the monitor. Billy is sitting up, his cries increasing.

"I think it's my turn," Frank says. He jerks himself to sit up and pulls the sheets off but is stopped by Laura.

"No, you have work in the morning. Make it up to me on the weekend," Laura says.

Frank lies back down. "God, I love you."

Laura sits up and hangs her feet over the side of the bed. She stretches out her arms over her head and lets out a massive yawn, her feet shivering. She slips into a nightgown and puts on her slippers, then, heads out, disappearing from Frank's sight, who lay peacefully in bed.

Laura turns on the light in Billy's room. He sits, blubbering in his crib, with his arms up in the air and hands grabbing in her direction. She walks to the crib.

"What's the matter, bubs?"

She picks him up and bounces him on her waist. He continues to cry.

"It's alright. It's alright. Momma is here."

She carries him over to a small rocking chair in the corner of the room and takes a seat. Cradled in her arms and looking up at her, Billy begins to calm as Laura gently rocks the chair. "There. There, bubs. Momma's here."

Billy's hands move around her face. Laura turns one of his little hands and rubs his palm with her thumb. Billy's fingers close over her thumb, gripping it tight. A large shadow fills the room and cascades over the two of them. Laura looks up from Billy.

"What are you doing, Frank?"

"I missed you."

"Missed me?" Laura smiles.

"Missed both of you."

Frank enters the room and gives Billy a kiss on the forehead and Laura, one on the lips. He sits on the floor next to the chair, with his hand over the arm stroking Billy's head. Billy's eyes bounce around the room from Laura to the ceiling to her hand. Then, his little voice drops a bomb. "Da...Da."

Laura's eyes beam with joy. Frank whips himself up to his knees in a delighted frenzy. He puts his hand on Laura's shoulder, looking down into Billy's eyes and holding his tiny palm in his. "Say it again, buddy!"

218

A Confession of Faded Flames

Winter 2031

*T*he casket is closed at the wake. Family and friends come and go. A small gathering line up at the cemetery for the funeral. Laura says her goodbyes, placing the toy plane amongst the flowers on top of the coffin. Ellis watches from far enough away to go unnoticed.

When the coast is clear, Ellis goes to Frank's grave, carrying a book. A mound of dirt sits a few feet away under a tarp. Billy's headstone neighbors a blank patch of grass where Frank's will eventually be placed.

"You know, one thing that place has protected me from is death," Ellis confesses. "Well, at least this whole process people go through. Buying expensive boxes to gift-wrap bodies in. Sitting in rooms full of heartache. Digging ditches in the ground. Marking them so those left behind can visit dust and bone. I can't say I understand it, or maybe I refuse to understand it, because nobody will ever do this for me. I'll either never die or be completely unknown when I finally do. I'm already a ghost. My former life was buried by time. It's a sick joke that I get an abundance of it, while you and Billy, and so many others, never get enough."

Ellis lifts the book he's holding, nervously playing with the dog ear on the corner of the cover. It's *The Time Machine*.

"I used to think one day that place would spit me out far enough into the future when real time machines finally existed. I'd dream about using one to go back and change things. Stop myself from shooting Bullet and following the blood trail. Give some younger version of myself a chance at living. Remove myself from every life I've altered. Make it so you and Laura never even met me. If after that, this me still remained, I would use the machine to rid the world of so much pain. Starting by saving your boy. But I don't know if I have it in me to wait that long." He tosses the book into the grave. "Not sure if you're even much of a reader, but it meant a lot to me and I want you to have it. I think that's as good as I can do for now."

A small backhoe approaches with two cemetery workers on board. They stop by the tarp and remove it from the dirt. "Take your time if you need it. We are in no rush," one of the workers says to Ellis.

"It's fine, I'm headed out."

Ellis marches from the cemetery straight into town. He stops at the gas station and purchases a one-gallon gas can along with a book of matches. He fills the can at the pump and walks off, back in the direction of Western Pass.

With determination, he follows the trails through the woods and into the clearing where JoJo awaits. Its naked branches sprawl out against the backdrop of a cloudy sky. Pointed fingers appearing ready to snatch Ellis from where he stands. His eyes are distilled. A choice has been made. Ellis twists the top off the can and proceeds in circles around the base to douse JoJo's trunk in gasoline. He splashes it furiously until there isn't a single drop left. Facing the front of the tree, he pulls the matchbook from his pocket and tears one from it. He strikes the match against the book, holds it for a couple of seconds and watches as it flickers. One last time, he savors the image of the place he called home for so long. Then, tosses the match at the tree.

The gasoline blazes along the roots and up the trunk, stopping at the height of where the gasoline reached. To Ellis's surprise, the flames don't crawl any higher. They don't spread across the ground. They burn the gasoline and the gasoline only. When there's no more fuel to burn, the flames die. JoJo remains unharmed.

Ellis charges the tree with a guttural scream and punches his fist into its trunk with all his might. The bark gouges the skin on his knuckles. He begins to bleed. He swings his other fist into the tree with matching results. One blow after another, he alternates slamming his fists into the tree until the pain is unbearable. He drops to his knees and leans his forehead against the tree, defeated. His splintered hands drip blood onto the ground. His anger subsides and he becomes despondent, crying in the snow.

How Big the Sky Was

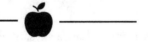

Fall 2028

*T*he playground is buzzing with sounds of children screaming their heads off. The line for the slide seems endless. A group of kids chase each other in a game of tag, nearly knocking over Laura, who pushes Billy on a swing.

"Higher!" Billy howls.

"Any higher and you'll touch the sun," Laura tells him. She pushes with a little more force.

Cutting through the early autumn wind, his little feet stretch him closer to the bright blue wonder above. "Daddy, I'm about to touch the sun," Billy shrieks, his little giggle rounding out the statement.

Frank watches in amusement from a bench. A small backpack shaped like an astronaut's helmet sits next to him. He uses his phone to snap a picture. Then, he digs through the backpack and takes out Billy's toy plane. Frank, with the plane in hand, runs toward Laura and

Billy mimicking flight sounds with his voice. He crashes it into Billy's stomach and wraps his arms around him in a hug, bringing the swing to a halt. Billy erupts in laughter.

"You're going to need to teach me how to land this thing," Frank says.

Billy takes the plane and hops off the swing.

"Mommy, can I go fly this with the other kids?"

"Be careful," Laura obliges.

Billy scampers off to a group of kids in a small field adjacent to the playground.

"Hey, mom. Need someone new to play with?" Frank asks. He flirtatiously winks at Laura and gives her a kiss. Her laughter settles into a bashful smile.

"Frank, not here," Laura says. Slightly embarrassed, she pushes his head away from hers.

He looks around and sees two other mothers watching them. When they catch Frank noticing, they pretend to mind their own kids. "They're just mad nobody's kissing them," Frank brags. He plants another wet kiss right on Laura's lips.

He takes her by the hand and walks her over to the same patch of grass where Billy and the other kids play. The two of them sit together, away from the noise. Laura points at Billy. "We made that, and it never doesn't blow my fucking mind. This little mixture of us running around, seeing so much for the first time."

"I used to be afraid of how big the sky was, you know," Frank says, putting his arm around Laura as she slinks into his embrace, "but I'm not anymore, and I think it's because I do a lot less looking up and worrying, and a lot more looking straight ahead at him and you...that's where the future lies...the one I want."

Laura entangles her fingers with Frank's as the sun begins to set along a pink horizon. "Promise we won't fuck this up," she says, a subtle desperation in her voice.

224

He looks into her eyes. Into that future.

"I promise."

A Bitter Lonely Cold

🍎

Winter 2031

*W*inter's door is coming to a close. Laura hadn't gone to the oak tree since the day at the hospital. Instead, she waits for the dead of night, after most of the world is asleep, and goes down to the playground. She sits in a swing, usually accompanied by some whiskey, until the cold becomes unbearable. On one such night, there is an older man, sleeping on a bench, his head laid back in the air. His many layers of clothing resemble a ball of fur. The breath fogs from his mouth.

Laura recognizes the man. "Martin?" she says, gently shaking him awake.

He's startled and almost trips himself off the bench.

"The people that like me call me, Moo."

Laura smiles to herself.

"Legs needed a rest. Must've fallen asleep. I'd be lying if I said I hadn't had a few already," he says.

Laura holds out her flask. Moo thanks her and takes a sip.

"Where are you headed at this hour?"

"Here," she says, walking to a swing and taking a seat.

"Weird place to be, in this weather."

"You're here."

He gets up to bring her the flask. "Exactly. I'm a fucking weirdo."

Laura chuckles under her breath. She takes the flask back and downs a huge gulp. Moo goes behind her and gives a tender push on the swing. "Don't let whatever got you here, turn you into me, kid," he says.

She motions the flask behind her head. He takes another swig and passes it back. He gives her one more push and comes back around front to bid farewell.

"Where are you off to now?"

"Oh, ya know, looking for people I lost in places I'll never find them," he says, tipping an imaginary hat in her direction.

Into the darkness he goes, leaving Laura alone. Her breath becomes more apparent the longer she stays. The tip of her nose purples as the snot begins to harden above her lip. She swings lightly, using the tips of her boots to draw random patterns in the snow. She looks over her shoulder and back again. There is nothing and her. The only voices are those locked within her mind and the language of the harsh winter air testing her fortitude.

Predictable Monsters

Winter 2031

*E*llis and Bullet sit under the apple tree, an open book in the young man's lap. His knuckles are wrapped in torn cloth, covered in blood. Most of the void's interior has decayed under lack of nourishment and the remnants of Sr.'s touch. Useless attempts to read are met with even more useless attempts to listen to music. Nothing can comfort Ellis. Nothing can keep his wandering mind off the horrors he took part in.

The weight of Bullet's imposing, opal eyes crush Ellis while he paces around in silence. "You don't know what it's like out there," Ellis unloads, "Watching broken people shuffle around. You don't see the beauty between the cracks either. You don't know what it feels like to give in again and have someone see you for you. Or, what it's like to want to do the right thing and only make it worse. You just sit there."

Now, facing Bullet, who sits expressionless in the only remaining speck of color, Ellis surrenders. "I know, finish the job," he whispers to himself.

***

It's a regular night at Rebels; low music and loud growls from patrons sitting at the bar top. Some commiserate in patches around tables and against the walls.

Moo stumbles into the bar.

Ellis, sitting alone at a table with his glass of coke, already has eyes on the old codger. Moo spots him and walks over.

"If you can remember my name, I'll let you buy me a drink," he jokes.

"Come on, Moo. Didn't think I'd forget about you," Ellis says. He helps Moo into his chair.

"Well, I'll be damned," Moo chuckles.

"Guess that means I like you," Ellis teases.

Moo's eyes grow sincere. "Guess it does, friend," he says, noticing Ellis's hand wraps, "Get into a fight?"

"Sort of. I didn't win."

"Tough break."

The old drunk flags the bartender down and motions with one finger in the air. He jumps off his chair to his feet, scratching his overgrown beard, and rummages through his pockets for some loose change. "Where is that jukebox?" he mumbles, his tired, red eyes searching for it across the bar. He shouts at the jukebox. "There ya-ar!" The dusty yellow light from its display illuminates his scraggly face. His cheeks are covered in freckles. The sides of his eyes wrinkled. "What was it, then?" he mutters to himself, flipping through the song choices. "Don't give me any clues now, Ellis. I'm gonna remember."

Ellis takes a sip from his drink as the bartender approaches with a glass of whiskey in his hand. Then, Moo's face engorges with delight. With force, he slaps the play button. "Leaving on a Jet Plane" comes on.

Moo slow dances his way to the table and points to his head.

"Told you I'd remember. Memory like an elephant. Ain't that right, Paulie?"

The bartender puts Moo's drink down on a coaster. "Maybe you can start remembering to pay your tab then, Dumbo."

Moo shrugs Paulie off and dances his way down into his seat. "I remember us sitting at this very table, bullshitting music and you saying this was your favorite song," Moo tells Ellis.

"Impressive," Ellis remarks.

Moo raises his glass, his hand trembling. "To my memory!"

Ellis lifts his soda. "To your memory."

They clink their glasses and take a stiff swig. The two of them drift into casual conversation. Moo carries on about how "shitty" the food is down at the shelter.

"I heard the eggs give you the runs," Ellis says, and then proceeds to order them late night grub from the bar: hamburgers and fries.

"Ya know, these are damned good fries. Not soggy at all," Moo rejoices. He holds one up in the air. "Paulie, how do you keep them crunchy, eyy?" He downs a handful more after drowning them in ketchup. "The drink. The food. Can you get me a job next?" Moo snorts with his mouth full.

Ellis indulges. "Hey, Paulie! Got a busboy opening for my friend?" Paulie rolls his eyes at the two of them and carries on rinsing some glasses. "I tried," Ellis says, shrugging his shoulders.

Moo sinks his teeth into the burger, talking while chewing. "Hard to keep a job. Last gig I had was years ago. Used to be a janitor at the Wyland Mall."

"What happened?"

"Don't remember it, but they said they found me threatening a shopper...can't always afford the meds, ya know?" Moo takes another bite of the burger. "I was accusing the guy of rape. Poor schmuck." He uses the last bit of the burger to collect all the ketchup and salt on the plate and swallows it. "Nobody believed me when I was a kid. About the man living below us. The secret games...sometimes I get real confused and see him in other people. Post Traumatic something or other some expensive shrink told me once. He's alive, ya know? The guy who did it. In a home. Dementia." Moo pauses at the thought, a bit lost in the air between them. He brings his attention back to his glass. "I've thought about going and killing him, ya know? At least I'd get a warm place to stay in prison."

"I am sorry, my friend. This world is full of animals," Ellis says.

"Eh, that's where you're wrong, Ellis. This world...it's full of humans. The most ordinary and predictable monsters." Moo takes a sip of his drink. "But, enough about my woes, Mr. Quiet. What's batting around between those eyes of yours? Something's stirring in there. You kids wear it right on your face. A parent knows. Lose someone? Heartache after a breakup? Kill someone and not sure where to bury the body?" Moo devilishly smirks at his last remark.

Ellis stiffens in his chair, then leans forward and waves Moo closer. "When I was a little boy, I got stuck between here and someplace else. Where time passes outside of it, but not within. JoJo. I'm bound to it. A gatekeeper. It thrives on pain and tragedy. Turns misery into masterpiece. But, when it runs out, when it becomes hungry again, it opens and spits me out into a world where the only thing that stays the same is heartbreak. And if I don't give it what it desires, it poisons me. Makes me catch up to the age I should be...," Ellis says. His face, made of stone. His tone, deadly serious.

Moo plays along. "Oh yeah, and what age would that be?"

"Too old to survive, I think."

Moo settles back in his chair. His finger circles the rim of his glass while he examines Ellis through a piercing stare. He lifts the glass, knocks back the remainder of his drink in one go, and falls into a fit of laughter. "And to think, they call me crazy. You're a fucking nut, my man!"

He only quietens when Ellis doesn't laugh along.

"So, this place between places...you wanna give it my pain?"

"I do," Ellis says.

At that moment, a man enters the bar wrapped up in a big coat and hat. He takes his hat off and stuffs it in one of the coat pockets. It's the burly, older man that had an outburst from when Ellis first met Laura at Rebels.

"Jack soda, Jay?" Paulie asks the man.

Jay ignores him and scans the room, a nervous jitter in his eyes. He holds his stare on Ellis.

Moo turns to follow Ellis's eyes, which are now on Jay.

"Ah, that quack. Likes to stir it up. Pay him no mind," Moo says.

Jay reaches a hand into his other coat pocket and advances toward their table. Ellis tenses up in his seat. Moo begins standing to cut him off.

"Okay, Jay. Let's not-," Moo says, before trading focus to Jay's coat pocket.

Jay pulls a revolver and points it at Ellis.

"For Clay," Jay says, his finger resting on the trigger.

Moo grabs his wrist and points Jay's hand to the sky as the gun goes off, the bullet entering the ceiling. Most of the crowd in the bar duck and cover. Ellis is frozen in his seat as Jay tussles with Moo. Before he can get the gun free to take another shot, two other men in the bar tackle Jay to the ground. He fights beneath them but their weight is too much for him to manage. Staring at Ellis, he shrieks, "He did this to me! He did this!"

One of the men pinning him down shouts to Paulie, "Call the cops!"

Moo slaps Ellis on the shoulder, "Come on pal. Let's get outta here before we gotta answer a bunch of fucking questions."

Watch the Boy

Summer 1942

*E*llis is asleep in a plain white crib, covered in a plain white blanket. He smiles in his sleep from a dream he's having. The room is sparse with faded blue paint on the walls. Curtain shadows dance in the splashes of sunlight pouring in from the windows. A few random toys are scattered across the hardwood floor. There are no pictures on the walls. No additional decor except for a rocking chair and dresser.

The sun shifts in the sky, and eventually beams directly into the crib, rustling little Ellis awake. He pulls himself up, wearing a cloth diaper. Clutching to the rails of the crib, he surveys the room. There is no one there except him. He cries out. Less than a minute passes and the door opens. In walks a gray-haired woman wearing a brown house dress. "Now, now, Ellie. Mee-maw is here," she says, shuffling herself to Ellis. With some effort she gets him out of the crib and rocks him in her arms. She gently rubs his back, whispering, "You hungry, my little one?" It doesn't quiet him.

Downstairs, with Ellis on her side, she heats up a baby bottle full of milk in a pot on the stove. His cries echo through the walls of the house. She sways with him, speaking in a soft voice to try and soothe his mood. "Almost, my little Ellie."

The front door flings open. Michael Foster enters, his hair wet from perspiring in the hot, summer sun. In his hands, he carries several bags of groceries. His clothes are dirty from a hard day's work. He brings the bags into the kitchen and places them on the counter. Greeting his mother cordially, he starts unpacking the bags.

"Pa...Pa...," Ellis says from his grandmother's arms. The boy reaches in the direction of his father. Michael continues with the groceries. His mother brings Ellis to him.

"I can tend to the groceries, Michael. You take Ellie."

Michael hesitantly takes Ellis in his arms. They stare into each other's eyes like two alien lifeforms seeing each other for the first time. "Pa," Ellis repeats.

In between filling the refrigerator, Michael's mother belts out instructions, "Michael, don't let it boil too much."

Michael turns the stove off and removes the baby bottle to let it cool down. He stands, unsure, in the middle of the kitchen. His mother stops her task at hand, dismayed. "Just go and sit on the couch with Ellis. I'll take care of it from here."

Michael listens and sinks into the couch with Ellis on his lap. Absorbed by his father's beard, his tiny fingers grab hold of a hunk of its wiry hair, pulling it slightly. Ellis then reaches for one of Michael's ears, tugging on the lobe. His little hand caresses across Michael's face. His father stiffens, grabs Ellis by the arms and plops the boy down on the cushion next to him. Michael's focus gravitates from Ellis to the urn on the mantle.

Mee-maw steps into Michael's view, motioning the baby bottle toward him. "Maybe it's best if you fed the boy."

"I have work to do out back," Michael suggests. He stands up from the couch.

"Michael, I am not going to be around forever. You're gonna have to take care of your son someday, ya know?"

Michael slips out the backdoor. Frustrated, his mother sits beside Ellis and hands him his bottle.

Amber light swallows the earth from a low sitting sun as Michael tends to a garden in the backyard. It nestles adjacent to the tall tree, full of bright, green leaves. On his knees, he plucks fresh tomatoes and cucumbers into a bucket. He pauses and removes a flask from his back pocket. He takes a swig, his eyes sweeping through the yard. The backdoor opens behind him, and he hurriedly stashes the flask back in his pocket. His mother exits the house with a pitcher of lemonade. Ellis hobbles out in front of her, carrying his almost empty bottle.

She sets the lemonade and two glasses down on a small bistro table. Then, proceeds to fill the glasses and walk one over to Michael, Ellis in tow. Michael stands to face them, the sweat seeping through his clothing. He grabs the glass and takes a healthy gulp.

Ellis trots aimlessly around the backyard, eventually losing his balance and plopping down in a shaded patch of grass. His chubby little fingers claw at the blades of grass. Michael and his mother watch from the small garden. She grabs the bucket from him. "I'll bring these in. Watch the boy, Michael," she says, stern in her command.

Michael has no choice. He finishes his lemonade with a second gulp and hands her the empty glass. His mother walks off, back into the house to put the vegetables away. Michael watches Ellis play in the dirt, his little body lost in the massive shadow of the tree.

Old Friends

Winter 2031

*T*he farther Ellis and Moo get from Rebels, the quieter Hollow Hills becomes. Moo comments on every landmark they pass that holds any importance to him.

"You see that church there?" Moo says, pointing to his left. "I had my first kiss with Amy Mason inside St. Sebastian's. We snuck up from the rec hall in the basement during a charity drive and necked in Father Middleton's confessional."

Ellis nods along.

"Outside Esterman's Deli, I got into my first fist fight. It was with Donny Grey, the local bully. He wouldn't stop picking on the younger kids. God, I was too hot-blooded then," Moo admits in a chortle. "I lost the fight, of course. Lied to my mother about the cuts and bruises. Said I was playing tackle football on the pavement with friends. She bought it."

They continue to wind through town, stopping in front of a school.

"Oh, and there! That is where I met my wife, Genevieve, when we were seventeen, on the front steps of Hollow Hills High School. She was the new kid, running late because she missed the bus. I was running late, well, because that's just what I did. We hit it off over our love for David Bowie." Moo's smile is short lived. "She left me long ago, though. The drinking. She passed some years ago."

Moo walks up a few of the school's steps. Ellis remains on the sidewalk.

"It was right here...," Moo says, somberly looking down at his feet, "Where I once held the whole fucking universe in my heart."

He returns to the sidewalk. Ellis throws an arm around his shoulder. "I have a hunch she's waiting for you on the other side of this existence, my friend."

They cross onto main street, and walk east toward the cliffs, stopping once more outside the playground. Its swings rock in the breeze, their rust creaking with a benign whistle.

"I used to come here sometimes when my dad worked. Only time I'd get a chance to, really," Ellis confides.

Moo takes a step inside the playground. "I still come here a lot. Reminds me of family," Moo admits. The drunkenness in his voice fades away at the thought.

"Family? Do you have kids? At the bar, you mentioned that a parent knows," Ellis prods.

Moo ignores the question.

"This is actually where you and I first met," Ellis admits, "You pushed me too high on a swing once, back in 1967. Your father tried to help me, and I ran. Then, years later, you told me about Cujo at the rental store you worked at. I read it, you know? It's a favorite and I want to thank you for introducing me to King. One other time-"

"You gave me money outside St. Sebastian's," Moo says,

turning back to face Ellis.

"You remember," Ellis says.

"I'd be lying if I said I remember them all throughout my life. But, right now, hearing you mention them, they each came back. I can see you as you are now, back then, on the sidewalk."

The two of them share a smile. Moo shakes his head in humored disbelief and turns back to face the empty playground. He steps in closer to the swing set. "You know I saw your friend up here the other night. The dirty blonde, who kicked me outta my seat."

"Laura?"

"Didn't catch her name. Up here drinking by herself. She seemed out of it. I could feel it. I could recognize it. That she was looking for the same thing I was. An end to all the bullshit." Moo savors a few seconds more, then turns back to the sidewalk. "So, JoJo, the fuck kinda name is that for a tree?"

Ellis is gone.

A Wanted Visitor

Winter 2031

*T*he Nagan house is quiet and dark. Laura sits, almost comatose, in the living room, staring at a blank TV, with an empty bottle of whiskey on the coffee table. She is in a haze, comfortable under the numb blanket of darkness in the room. An abyss with no magic, no altered reality, or reanimated ghosts. Just her and what's real - the pain. A knock at the door jostles her nerves. She is visibly annoyed but gets up to answer it. It's Ellis.

"Why are you here, Ellis?"

"I wanted to see you one last time. To make sure you're okay and to say I am sorry for having gotten you involved. There isn't much time left if you want to see Billy before it closes up again."

"No more talking about that place. Please, no more. It's too much, Ellis."

"Okay, I'll go."

"No, you're already here. Come in."

Ellis steps inside.

"Hungry?" she asks.

In the kitchen, food from neighbors is stacked all over the island. Unopened sympathy cards are scattered about one of the countertops next to a first aid kit. Ellis fixes himself a plate from the grief food, his hands now properly wrapped with gauze. He offers to spoon some of the anti-pasta into Laura's dish. She declines and rustles through the refrigerator, pulling out a casserole dish.

"These fucking neighbors don't stop bringing this shit. I don't get it. We never talk. It's only me here to eat this all. So, now I'm burdened with the cleanup and returning their Tupperware...it's just more punishment," she chafes.

Laura removes the lid of the casserole dish and empties the contents onto her plate. Roasted potatoes, Brussels sprouts, three bean salad, and a small chunk of salmon. "Frank was an amazing cook, and this is all that's left of the last thing he ever made." She snags a forkful of three-bean salad and eats it before putting the plate in the microwave and turning it on. "When we were dating, Frank bought a painting from my first ever showing. Told me he ate nothing but beans for weeks to be able to afford it."

"How did you two meet?" Ellis asks.

"I was interning at a gallery in the city. He was a carpenter's assistant on a reno of the flooring in the art space. He was always early to work. Took me a while to realize it was because he had a thing for me and wanted more time to chat me up. I thought he was funny and cute. I liked that he took his job seriously and was good at it. The last day of the job, he finally had the courage to ask me out. We went for a coffee after my shift and that was that," she reminisces. The microwave beeps. Laura takes the hot plate out and quickly puts it down to keep from burning her fingers.

"Sounds like a perfect thing. What happened?"

Laura laughs, "Really just going for it, huh?" She grins, munching on a potato from her plate. Ellis is embarrassed.

"A lot and a little happened. Sometimes the little seemed to do more damage. All these ignored, minute details stack and stack and stack. If you never decide to do anything about them, the bottom eventually gives out. You become antagonistic toward one another on the freefall. Pushing buttons. Talking less. Touching less. A million little moments comprise most demises, Ellis. And then, when we lost Billy, we lost everything."

Ellis opens his mouth to ask another question.

Chewing on some salmon, Laura cuts him off. "Enough about me. What's on your mind?"

Without thinking, Ellis replies, "Love."

Laura lowers a potato from her mouth. "What about love?"

"It's an alien concept to me. How it operates. I hear you talk about it with Frank. Marie about James. How could something meant to be so good constantly become so tragic? I want it, but I also don't," he divulges.

Laura hesitates a moment to collect her thoughts. "You're looking at it all wrong, Ellis. Marie and James are not a tragic story. Their love lasted their entire lives. Her sadness for him, like mine for Billy and Frank, are proof people can have profound effects on us. Even yourself, the way you miss Marie. True love comes with the understanding that there will be pain when you lose those you share it with."

"Maybe that's why I fear having to say goodbye to you and I feel awful admitting that," he says, unable to look her in the eyes.

"I'm flattered, Ellis. Truly. But sometimes fondness for people sprouts from circumstance. Who besides me have you had the opportunity to fall for?"

Ellis fiddles with his fork in some macaroni on his plate.

"Love is a storm we can't predict and should never shelter

from," he says.

"Which book of yours is that from?"

Search for the Lover

Winter 2015

*J*oJo grows hungry enough to open again. Ellis proceeds to pack his backpack, stuffing it with borrowed books and spare clothes. He mends his torn shoes and steps into the outside world. The leaves throughout the trails have all found the ground in various stages of rust - fleshy reds, faded oranges and yellows, and cracked, broken browns. The stream is much louder, its ripples finding their ways between the empty branches to Ellis's ears.

He takes a detour toward the loudest parts of the stream, where the water tumbles its way through larger stones and rocks, cascading down a miniature waterfall. Bending down, he cups his hand to collect some water and drink it. It's refreshing. He sips a bit more from his hand and then wipes his palm dry along his pants.

Standing again, he surveys past the collection of rocks to where the stream is a bit wider and calm. In the distance, a family of deer drink from the water. The stag senses Ellis and turns to face him. The span of its massive antlers is impressive to the once young hunter. It moves around the other side of its fawn to safeguard it from Ellis's presence. "It's okay, pops. I don't mean no harm," Ellis says to himself, before continuing back the way he came.

***

Nothing much has changed in the cemetery, except a few new tombstones had homes. Ellis cleans the dried leaves from the front of his father's grave and takes a seat in the grass. "Just saw a big one. You would've made a trophy from the points."

Ellis readjusts his position to lean back on his palms and stretch his legs out toward the tombstone. He looks up into the sky, which is struggling to decide whether it wants to be blue or gray. "I think, this time, I'm going to look for a man that was once in love and see if I can give it back to him."

***

At the library, Ellis returns older books to a much younger librarian. He tells her the same fib, that he found them in his mother's house after she passed. It works. He takes his sweet time searching the shelves for what strikes him and brings them back to the librarian's desk.

"Eclectic choices," she says as she scans the books.

"For some, it's the cover. Others, it's the title. Often, it's by how interesting I find an author's name. I don't want to know too much. I trust my gut and let them all be a special surprise," he says.

The librarian smiles. "I like that!"

***

Ellis makes his way east to drop by his old house. It's still brand new and appears to be inhabited by the same happy family. The tree in the backyard has grown stronger by the years, shading almost the entire house with its branches. Nobody seems to be home, so he hops the fence into the backyard.

An above ground pool takes up most of the yard. A modern day shed occupies one corner against the fence. The tree's trunk is massive. He approaches and places his hand on the bark. Nothing happens. It doesn't open. No mysterious gateway to punishment. No silent animal to lead him in. It is simply a tree. "I wish I knew you. I wish we could have watched each other grow," he says.

A neighbor behind the tree opens their sliding glass door and steps out onto the deck in their backyard. The man is older and squints at Ellis. His concern grows and he begins to walk down the steps, into his yard toward the fence nearest the tree. Ellis doesn't hesitate and exits the way he came, quickly hopping the gate and darting down the street.

Back in town, he avoids going to Rebels and instead wanders the streets in his search for the man who was once in love. He enters businesses one-by-one, day after day, returning to and from the void throughout winter trying to solve the mystery of *C.A. + J.L. 5/13/57.*

Find the Lover

Winter 2015

*I*n late February, on an exceptionally cold Sunday, Ellis takes cover in St. Sebastian's to keep warm. He sits towards the back, closer to the votive candles; a scattered few were lit. Not many people are in attendance, bodies taking up minimal space amongst the pews. A middle-aged priest walks to the pulpit on the altar to carry out mass. Everyone in the church follows his lead.

The door to the church squeals open, temporarily halting the mass. A man hurries down the center aisle, apologizing to the congregation. He walks past Ellis and takes a seat toward the front of the church. It's him, the man who sat outside JoJo and cried. The hair on his head has receded further and his beard a tad bushier, but Ellis is certain it is him.

Dutiful in his beliefs, the man is dressed in his Sunday best, reciting all the prayers by heart, giving all the proper "Amens" and

"Hallelujahs" when prompted. He kneels, when necessary, and waits graciously in line for his turn to get communion and wine. He grants everyone peace around him when the priest requests the congregation to do so. He even volunteers as an usher and walks around with one of the collection baskets when it's time for donations, to which Ellis spares five dollars.

When mass ends, the man is greeted by some of the other attendees. They share pleasantries and fall into a conversation Ellis can't quite hear, occasionally bursting into laughter. In due time, the small crowd disperses onto the sidewalk. Everyone gets into their cars and bids farewell. The man takes off alone into town. Ellis heads in the same direction but is stopped by a beggar outside the church.

"Spare a little something, pal," the man says. He is bundled up in shoddy clothes, his mustache stiff from the cold. Ellis can't help but take pause and look into the man's eyes. It's the boy that pushed him on the swing, the young man that tried to rent him a movie, and the drunk that bumped into him at Rebels. Ellis pulls a few dollars from his pocket and hands it to the man. "Don't spend it all in one place, Moo."

Moo's eye's grow puzzled. "I don't know you. How do you know that name?"

"In a town like this, you just pick up on things over the years," Ellis says.

Moo tips his hat in thanks.

Ellis hurries off in the direction of the man from the church. He catches up as the man stops by Esterman's Deli and purchases a newspaper. Ellis pauses by a tree where the phone booth Marie used once stood. The man continues down the street into the Roundabout Diner on the following corner.

Inside, the hostess seems to recognize the man and gives him a seat in a booth alongside a window that faces the street. She brings him a coffee. He smiles and nods, then starts reading the paper.

252

Ellis enters and is greeted by the cheery hostess; her name tag reads: *Cassandra*. "Can I help you with something, sir?" she asks, contorting her face to investigate Ellis a bit closer. "Do I know you, hon?"

Ellis shakes his head. "I'm meeting with a friend that is already here."

Cassandra lets him pass and enter the main dining area. Ellis sweeps the room for the man and spots him at the booth, the newspaper covering his face. Ellis goes to the man's table and settles into the booth bench opposite him, prompting him to lower the newspaper. Confused, the man asks, "Can I help you?"

"Are you C.A. or J.L?" Ellis asks.

"Pardon," the man gasps.

"The initials you carved on that tree out in the woods when you were young. You'd come and have picnics with that woman."

The man folds the paper completely and pushes it to the side as the waitress puts down a plate of eggs and hash browns. "Thank you, Cassandra!"

"You're welcome. Does your new friend here want anything, Mr. Lyons?" she asks, as she places his utensils next to the plate of eggs. The man looks at Ellis to reply to the question himself.

"I'm full, thank you," Ellis says.

"Okay, sweetie. Sorry, but it's really bothering me. Are you sure I don't know you? Did you have a father by the name of...Ellis? I swear you look like someone I used to work with," Cassandra says.

"No, my father's name was Michael."

"The darndest thing," Cassandra says. She walks off to take another table's order.

"Mr. Lyons?" Ellis questions.

"Jonathan Lyons," admits the man in utter disbelief.

"And the woman?"

"Cathy Aldridge."

Mr. Lyons rubs his forehead in thought, then lowers his hand to his mouth. "How could you possibly know about us?"

Give the Lover Love Again

Winter 2015

*M*r. Lyons and Ellis stand in the clearing before the oak tree; the four letters etched into its bark stare back at them. "Back then, we couldn't be comfortably out in the open as a couple," Mr. Lyons says, approaching the letters. "So, we hid here that summer as much as we could, until her father found out, and forbade us from seeing each other. He sent her away to live with her mother on the other side of the country. We tried to keep in touch. Sent letters. But time moved on and we both eventually found other people. Started families that weren't the ones we thought we would. We met one time as adults when she was back in town for her father's funeral. Kissed in the rain. Said goodbye."

The emotions bubble to the surface and plant a smile on his face. "I told my wife about it. She was heartbroken. We separated. Then, that day, two years ago, Cathy was being buried somewhere I couldn't afford to travel to. So, I came here...the only place that had any signs of what we had together," he explains, the sadness alive again in his voice.

Ellis places his hand over the letters in the bark and the doorway opens as it always does. Mr. Lyons is stupefied, his jaw hung low in disbelief.

"Come inside, Mr. Lyons. Welcome to JoJo."

He leads Mr. Lyons inside. Bullet sits under the apple tree, acknowledging the new presence.

"Bullet, he's trapped in here, too," Ellis says. He watches Mr. Lyons take in the half-colored landscapes around him.

"Why JoJo?"

"I don't know. Just a name I made up as a kid."

"Okay, and what exactly is this place?"

"Like I told you on the way over, a magical prison I can't get away from. It survives on grief, which then allows me to survive," Ellis reiterates. He plucks a green apple and tosses it to Mr. Lyons. "You're going to need this in order to take the trip."

The man catches it, rolling the apple around in his palm. "If I know one thing, it's that eating an apple from a magic tree doesn't typically end well. But, if what you say is possible, then what is there to lose?"

Bullet acts as an usher, leading someone from the ripples of the apple tree. The outline of a woman Mr. Lyons recognizes steps into focus. "Cathy?"

Ellis eyes the apple in Mr. Lyons' hand. The man quickly bites into it and lets the heavenly flavor settle into his bones. Cathy walks over and embraces him, stroking his white hair and holding him in her arms. His tears drip color into the blueprint of her form, until she is a blazing rainbow. They release their grasp. He holds her face in his hand, never averting. He smiles from ear to ear, radiating a flood of emotions. "I can still hear our songs, Cathy. I can still hear you." She takes his hand and walks him to the apple tree.

Ellis watches on as he always does, but his eyes sink as he second guesses himself. "You don't have to go. Maybe this is a mistake. I could be wrong about what's on the other side. You could visit her for the rest of the winter instead. Make up your mind later."

Mr. Lyons turns back to Ellis. "Love is a storm we can't predict and should never shelter from, Ellis. And boy, do I regret sheltering from it. Nothing could convince me to return to a world that once believed we should not be in love. Wherever she is, is the Heaven I want to be a part of," Mr. Lyons concludes, before vanishing into the unknown with Cathy by his side.

Tiny Seeds of Hope

Winter 2031

*S*everal abstract portraits on the floor line one side of the studio. One is a candid portrait of Frank leaning over Billy fast asleep in his crib, smiling. Laura hesitates in front of it and keeps her thoughts to herself, a fondness in her eyes. She removes various colors of paint from a pantry in the corner and brings them to the center counter in the room. "Ellis, could you grab two easels and blank canvases from over there?"

Ellis gathers the easels, sets them up, and places a blank canvas on each one. Then, he takes it upon himself to grab a small cup of brushes for the two of them. Laura finishes blotting the colors onto wooden palettes. "There you go. You're all set," she says.

On the other side of the counter, Laura starts right in.

Ellis contemplates his. Lost in the blank canvas, he says, "I've never painted before."

Laura laughs. "You've spent your entire life painting! You are unlike any artist I have ever seen. You know exactly what to do."

Ellis smirks, considering the thought. He picks up his brush, stroking the hairs to get a better feel of it before gently dipping it in some red paint. He watches Laura while she is immersed in her own creation and muses on the candid nature of her peace in the moment. He is patient with his brushstrokes, careful to form her outline just right. He focuses extra time on her eyes, going over them until they appear as deeply involved as hers do on her own painting. By the time he is done, she is illuminated with every color from his palette.

Laura sticks to the abstract. Her canvas is a scattershot of color. Bright tones bleeding through dark ones. Splats landing in involuntary patterns across a landscape of turmoil. A white horizon line stretches from left to right with different size figures of yellow and green moving toward it. Ellis watches her in awe. She has paint on her cheek and forehead, some even in her hair. She makes the final strokes carefully, and shouts, "Voila!"

They turn their creations toward one another. Laura is awestruck at her image on Ellis's canvas.

"Two versions of the same life," Ellis remarks.

"I see hope in them. Tiny seeds of hope in the darkness," Laura says.

She hangs both side-by-side on the wall opposite her other paintings. The two of them spend a few minutes in silence, studying each other's work.

"You look alive when you paint," Ellis says.

"So, you're saying I look like a corpse all the rest of the time, Ellis? Real nice," Laura jokes.

"No...it's just...you...," Ellis stutters, trying to form words to convey what he feels.

She puts her hand on his shoulder. "I'm kidding. You're right. I do."

Their eyes entangle. Ellis's Adam's apple fluctuates in his throat. Laura smiles and turns to view their paintings, rubbing some extra paint off her corners.

Ellis glances at his watch. "It's really late. I should go."

"Ellis, it's two in the morning. You're not walking all the way back there and I, sure as shit, am not driving you." Laura removes her hand from his shoulder and heads for the exit. At the door, she turns back, "Plus, it will feel nice to have someone else in the house. I don't want to be alone."

Laura prepares the guest bedroom for Ellis. It doesn't take long after he crawls into bed for his eyes to get heavy and close, a visiting glimmer of Bullet in his mind's eye as he slips into a deep sleep.

A darkness, this empty body awaiting love. There are no stars in the sky. No amber morning warmth. Voiceless. Sunken beneath the eerie weight of non-existent eyes and the phantom touch of people who aren't there. A lineage barely holding on. Survival. Two as one. Silence and the breach of light. Mouth hungry for milk. Eyes wide with creation. Innocence in the hands of nature. Breath of life into unknown places. A fawn set for streams of future violence and homes of nowhere with the carrier of death. Blood and snow kissing holes into the quiet bark of forgotten trees. Teeth of mystery open for business. Try to find a difference between Gods and dogs. I am felt and unseen. Not the air but some nothing wrapped softly around the love and tragedy it carries. Flickers of light and hell in hidden seams. My hand to the world, warm thuds speak from its chest. Bursting, vibrating, this heart of wandering beasts. Refuse time. Give me the agony and ache of flesh and marrow. The tears of broken dreams and taste of past hauntings. Half-dead animals find comfort in the colors of all this delicate fear. Grieve in my gullet and court the pangs of strangers. Bind the poison of loneliness to the places they cannot see, away from the horrors of human behavior. Pulse of the Earth is its name. Gatekeeper to vanishing acts and tapestries; to timeless gardens and other beautiful miseries.

Ellis awakens to a loud thud against the floor above him. He sits up in bed and listens intently. The sound of feet can be heard shuffling across the floor, followed by a muffled Laura. "Shit!"

Ellis exits his room and walks upstairs. He finds Laura in a white nightgown, scrambling in the hallway to gather model planes back into a cardboard box at the foot of an attic staircase that's been lowered. Behind her, the door to Billy's room is open and the lights are on. Ellis helps her re-pack the planes in the box.

"Sorry for waking you."

"No, it's fine."

Ellis takes the box up into the attic.

"Just put it anywhere, for now," Laura instructs from below.

He sets the box among others marked "Bubs Room". The fresh smell of sharpie stings his nostrils. He climbs down and asks Laura how he can help. She takes him into Billy's room which is partially emptied. The bed has no sheets on it. All the posters have been removed from the walls. Most shelves have been cleared of their toys. Flattened cardboard boxes are stacked against a wall.

"I couldn't sleep. So, I came in here and...," Laura struggles to get the words out.

"I couldn't sleep either," Ellis says, grabbing one of the boxes and folding it open. "Where should I start?"

Laura points to a small desk. "I still have to clear the drawers in there. You can do that while I go through the closet."

Ellis begins clearing the drawers out. Laura takes another box to the closet and starts removing clothing from hangers and neatly placing them into it. The desk is mainly filled with random action figures, sticker books, and various battle card games. Ellis empties all but one drawer into the box, seals it, and grabs another. He opens the bottom drawer. To his surprise, it is lined with cassette tapes. On top of the cassettes is a tape player with headphones plugged into it. He removes the player and examines it.

"He loved that thing," Laura says from across the room.

"Don't kids nowadays have swipy phone computers for music?" Ellis asks.

Laura laughs at him. "It's my mother's. She gave it to him and it automatically became the 'BEST way to listen to music, mommy.'"

Ellis pops the player open and removes the tape inside. It's *Album 1700* by Peter, Paul and Mary. The sight renders Ellis speechless, his eyes glistening over with nostalgia of better days. He pushes the tape back in and walks to Laura at the closet. Holding the headphones up, he positions one to her ear, which she holds in place, and then the opposite headphone against his own, and presses play. "Leaving on a Jet Plane" emits in a low volume between them. They both listen as if their life depended on it.

Early into the song, Ellis takes the headphones and puts them on Laura's head so she can enjoy the entirety of it. Then, he collects her hands in his and begins to dance. Laura smiles through her tears, moving her hands around his shoulders and placing his on her waist. An unspoken peace lives in the air between their eyes. Laura rests her head into the comfort of Ellis's chest. The two of them hypnotically sway; Ellis in the silence of the room, and Laura to the song. The song comes to an end and Laura removes the headphones. Ellis takes them from her and goes to place them in a box.

"No," Laura says.

Ellis pulls them back out. "You're right, no harm in keeping some of the things out."

"No. There's no point in packing any of it away," she speculates.

"But you're making such great progress, Laura. This is a huge step."

Laura sits on the edge of the bed. "If I pack it away, then the walls will haunt me. If I tear them down, I'll hear them both in the silence. If I move away, grief will find its way into my luggage. Sadness doesn't give a fuck about distance."

Ellis sits beside her on the bed. "What are you saying, Laura?"

She turns to face him and, with full conviction, says, "I want to go into whatever awaits on the other side of your void, Ellis."

"But, what if...,"

"Stop. Don't try to talk me out of it, Ellis. I'm sure," she insists.

Ellis respects her request and doesn't push the subject. The two of them sit in the silence. He scans the room as he thinks and can't help but notice a family photo left on a dresser across the room - Billy, smiling and happy, in Laura's arms.

Laura follows his eyes to the photo.

The question takes shape in his mind and falls from Ellis's mouth like a tidal wave. "Who did it?"

A Girl and Her Cow

November 22, 2031

*I*t's a Saturday morning. Radiant sunshine blasts through curtains, illuminating a sophisticated and tidy bedroom. Rose Whitley wakes to her daughter, Meadow, jumping on the bed, clutching a stuffed cow, screaming, "Pancakes!"

Meadow is a tiny girl full of energy with long brown hair and a face full of freckles. Rose interrupts her jumping and pulls her down to the mattress, tickling her. Meadow laughs hysterically.

"Banana or blueberry?" Rose asks.

"Blueberry!" Meadow shouts between a flurry of tickles.

At the kitchen counter, Meadow chomps away at her breakfast, talking between chews about her excitement for her birthday. Her cow sits on top of the table in front of the chair beside her. Amidst her constant chatter, she throws hints to Rose about what she wants.

"I was thinking if you can't get the rainbow sneakers, maybe just a rainbow poster!"

"Be patient, Meds. And eat with your mouth closed. It's good manners," Rose tells her.

Rose's cell phone rings. She looks at the screen, it displays the name "Paul". Rose rolls her eyes and takes it to the living room to answer. "Do I even need to ask why you're calling two hours before you're supposed to pick up your daughter?" She listens quietly for a minute, pacing furiously. "You're a real piece of work. I honestly don't have time for this, Paul." She hangs up.

Rose takes a deep breath before going back into the kitchen, where Meadow sops a chunk of pancake in maple syrup. "Hey, kiddo. Dad can't make it today. He had something come up that he can't get out of. I'm sorry," Rose admits, swallowing the sour taste in her mouth.

Meadow grows sullen.

Rose acts fast. "What if we went and got you an early birthday gift? Have us a girls' day."

***

At the mall, the two of them shop at all their favorite stores. Meadow gets new light up sneakers and a poster of her favorite YouTube gamers. They eat their favorite junk at the food court. Rose even splurges for the overpriced tickets to the Ferris Wheel. Together, they yell when their seats stop at the top. It catches everyone's attention. The two of them laugh. Meadow spots a boy, Billy, staring up from below.

Rose and Meadow grab some ice cream for the ride home. Chocolate-chip cookie dough for Rose; one scoop of vanilla and one scoop of chocolate, topped with rainbow sprinkles for Meadow. Rose tosses their shopping bags in the trunk of the car. Meadow gets fastened into the backseat. Rose gets in, starts the car, and checks the rearview mirror to make sure all is clear before backing out. A right turn, then a tight left around a few cars to approach the exit, where the light at the gate turns from green to yellow. Rose accelerates to catch it. Meadow drops her spoon on the floor. "I can't reach it, Mommy."

Rose reaches behind her seat to fish the spoon off the floor but can't feel it. She turns her head to get eyes on it. When she turns back, there is a little boy with a plane stepping into her view. The brakes screech. The thud chills her to the bone.

"What happened?" Meadow's voice reaches Rose's ears, but she can't answer through the shock. Rose watches as Laura falls to the ground in horror, picking Billy's lifeless body up into her arms. Their eyes meet. Rose gasps in despair.

Laura cries for help. "Someone call 9-1-1!"

People start to surround the accident. Many go to console Laura. A few stand outside Rose's car, shouting. She is frozen. Her hands remain on the steering wheel, trembling. She begins to breathe rapidly, hyperventilating. The only thing nearby is Meadow's stuffed cow, which has landed on the front seat. Rose grabs it as hard as she can and squeezes it into her chest as she rocks back and forth, her breathing increasing.

"Mommy, are you okay?"

A stranger opens the driver's side door and attempts to calm them. Rose's eyes remain fixated on the tragedy before her. The ambulance arrives and departs. The police arrive and depart. In the commotion, Rose can't speak with Laura before she gets into the ambulance with her son. Lawyers call. Lawsuits mount. Reporters and cops knock on the door. Friends don't pick up the phone. What little family she has offers food and platitudes. Pill and wine bottles begin to collect. She takes the bus to work now. Meadow hardly recognizes her. Paul tells her he is going to file for full custody.

A Mother Lost

Winter 2031

*T*he morning of the boy's funeral, after a string of nights with no sleep, Meadow leaps on Rose's bed for breakfast, but Rose hardly reacts. Catatonic from exhaustion, she is unable to look in her daughter's eyes. Meadow persists and a zombified version of her mother shuffles into the kitchen. Rose pours Meadow a bowl of cereal and places a glass of orange juice beside it.

"Pancakes!" Meadow yells.

"Not today."

"But I want banana pancakes."

"It's cereal or nothing, Meds."

Meadow scoffs under her breath and takes the bowl of cereal to the living room to eat over some cartoons. Rose walks to the sliding glass door in the family room and peers out into the backyard. The sky is gray and cloudy, the cold air swirling around barren trees. In the center of the yard, she hallucinates a tiny coffin surrounded by people dressed in black. Laura stands over the coffin, inconsolable.

Rose opens the door and is hit with a gust of wind that snatches the breath from her lungs. With it comes the wailing of the devastated mother. The funeral delusion pulls Rose outside into the bitter cold, barefoot.

"Mommy, close the door. It's getting cold," Meadow barks out, without taking her eyes off the TV.

Rose is fixated on the burial. Her eyes spill oceans and her feet begin to blue from the frigid temperatures. She clutches her chest in agony. "I'M SORRY! I'M SO SORRY! TAKE ME! TAKE ME!"

Meadow hears the commotion. At the open door, she spots her mother in the yard, on her knees, screaming into the blistering air at nothing. "Mommy!"

An older neighbor, sweeping the walk along the side of the adjacent house can hear the shrieks. He lowers his broom and peers over the fence. Rose continues to unravel, with Meadow crying at the back door.

Inside her kitchen, Rose sits covered in a blanket, while her neighbor pours some hot tea into a mug. "Thank you, Walt." Rose wraps her freezing fingers around the mug to keep warm.

Walt's wife attempts to distract Meadow in the family room, but it does very little to take her attention off her mother. Her curious and concerned eyes peer through the doorway at Rose and their neighbor, but she can't quite hear what they're saying.

"I could see them all mourning around his little coffin. It seemed so real. I see that little boy everywhere I look. Even in my dreams, I can't escape what I've done," Rose explains, despondent.

"It was an accident, Rose." Walt gets up and brings the teapot back to the stove. Rose's color begins to return. "It was something you can't take back," Walt continues, "That's the hard truth of it. But you got yourself your own little girl, right in there, who needs you.

Whatever the fallout, you gotta deal with it. You can't also ruin her life. And I ain't gonna be around every time you decide to go screaming in the backyard like a banshee. Lucky it was me and not one of these other busybodies who woulda called the cops. I know this shit is easier said than done. You are in remarkable shoes with what you're facing and you ever feel it's too much, you come knock on our door or give us a call, okay?"

His kindness forces Rose to smile through her shame. "I feel like the plague. Nobody wants to be around the woman who ran over a kid."

"Where's your folks?" Walt asks.

The question causes Rose to sink back into herself.

Walt changes course. "Whelp, now you're stuck with Janice and me. How about you go get yourself cleaned up and we all have us some lunch?"

She does and they do, the four of them.

**

Rose is more present that week. She prepares a full breakfast for Meadow each morning. Walt and Janice check on her every day, often sharing dinner together. She even manages to keep most of the house neat to remain distracted. Saturday soon arrives for Paul to pick up Meadow.

"Paul," Rose says as she opens the door.

"Meadow, ready to go?" Paul asks from across the room, avoiding eye contact with Rose.

"Yes, daddy. Can I bring my coloring books?" Meadow asks, as she stuffs her bag with all her toys and crayons.

"You can bring whatever you want, Meds! Don't forget Moose," he says.

"It's Moo," corrects Rose, "and I put him in her duffle."

Meadow runs up to her dad, places her hand in his and heads out the door towards the car. She waves frantically from the car as Paul exits the driveway. Rose waves back, as do Walt and Janice from the porch next door.

"Why don't you come and stay the weekend with us? We've got an exciting lineup of naps scheduled," Walt shouts to Rose.

Janice shakes her head behind him. "We are old, but not THAT old!"

"I appreciate the offer, but I want to see if I can be alone," Rose replies.

Rose keeps busy with chores, has an appetite, even laughs at a show on TV for a little bit. When the sun goes down, she buries herself in a book. The house is uncomfortably quiet. She only lasts a few pages and puts the book down.

Upstairs, in Meadow's room, she straightens up toys and changes the sheets on the bed. The closet is ajar. Rose goes to close it, but stops herself, and opens it instead. She thumbs through Meadow's clothes, randomly choosing a dress or sleeve to smell. She takes a shirt off its hanger and lies down on Meadow's bed with it. She spends the rest of the weekend there, alternating between a numb quiet and uncontrollable sadness.

Time continues as it always does and, on some days, Rose plays chicken with a handful of pills, or stares at knives much too long before chopping vegetables. But, then on other, rare days, Meadow and her carry about like they used to. Text messages and phone calls from friends return in the spotty "Hey" and "How are you?". When she's feeling brave, she takes Walt for a drive around the neighborhood. This is her life for a steady course of time. Two steps forward and five back.

An Act of Forgiveness

Winter 2031

*O*ne Sunday, while Rose is putting away dishes, the doorbell rings. When she opens the door, there stands a man in a long winter coat and polished boots, with his hands in his pockets. His brown scarf covers the lower half of his face, matching his exposed eyes.

"Can I help you?" Rose asks.

The man unwinds the scarf from his face. Rose recognizes him.

"Rose Whitley? I'm Frank Nagan."

Rose is locked in fear and can't utter a word.

"My apologies for stopping by unannounced. I wouldn't if I didn't feel it imperative we speak," Frank explains earnestly.

"Who are you?" Meadow questions from her mother's waist.

"Hey, there! I'm Frank," he responds in a kid-friendly voice.

"It's an old friend, Meds. Get back inside from the cold."

Meadow begrudgingly listens. Rose steps outside and closes the door behind her, wrapping herself tighter in her robe. "I'd rather not do this around her."

"I understand," Frank replies.

The two of them step into the garage. Rose closes the door behind them and immediately turns red with guilt. Her nerves are an earthquake to her body. The ache in her heart hangs on every word that leaves her mouth as she performs a self-exorcism.

"I wish I could trade places with him. Every single day, I wish it were me in that cemetery. Sorry is such an empty, pathetic word to use. All words are, it seems. If there was one in the dictionary that could carry the weight of how sorry I was, I promise I'd use it. But nothing I say brings him back. Nothing I could possibly do, brings your boy back. I am prepared for whatever punishment you feel is right. I wish I were dead."

Frank interrupts. "Don't say that. Any of that. If it were to come true, you'd be leaving behind that beautiful girl of yours." He takes a deep breath and gets to why he came. "My wife, Laura, she wrote a suicide note the other night. She didn't go through with it, thankfully. But...it made everything sort of come into focus again. The grief has been so heavy for us, and I want her to be alright. To even begin to get there, it all must be done with. This whole debacle. We didn't even want to file a lawsuit, you know, but we were lost and gave into outside pressure from family."

"I'd sue me," Rose admits, stepping closer to Frank. "I'd probably do much worse."

"We had an intense fury toward you, I won't lie about that. But...," he looks to her, his eyes full of grace, "we aren't the only ones suffering."

Rose chokes back the lump in her throat.

"It was a mistake. A moment that can't be undone...I forgive you."

The emotions swell in Rose. She bursts.

"Laura, I know she would too, but she has to work on forgiving herself first."

Rose sniffs back snot and rubs her face with the sleeve of her robe.

"I think the two of you ought to do that for yourselves, because guilt will eat away at you. I know. I let it ruin my relationship with the love of my life. Don't let it shorten yours."

Rose remains still in the center of the garage.

"Well, I better get going now."

Rose follows him out. They exchange a farewell and Frank gets into his truck. She watches him pull off and vanish around a bend in the road. Her lungs exhale a deep cloud of relief that disappears into the chill of winter.

Feeding Time

———— 🍎 ————

Winter 2031

*L*aura lay alone in Billy's bed come morning. Her eyes open and she covers them to keep the glare from blinding her. "Ellis," she calls out to no answer.

She sits up and calls for him again. No reply. There is no sign of him in the hallway or her bedroom. She even peers up into the attic with no luck. She ventures down the stairs and at the bottom of the stairwell, indistinguishable noises fade outward from the living room.

"Ellis," Laura beckons with concern.

In the living room, Ellis contorts wildly on the floor. His hands pressed tight to his stomach; he struggles through the pain. She drops to his side.

"Winter's end," he mumbles.

Laura grabs clean clothes from the Goodwill bags in her bedroom closet and gets him dressed. With his arm draped over her neck, she helps him into the garage and lies him down on the backseat of her car. Before she gets in, she notices the car isn't plugged into the charger. "Fuck," she says.

She helps Ellis back out of her car and walks him to the other side of the garage where Frank's truck is parked. The front end is still all chewed up. Laura leans Ellis against the bed of the truck and opens the driver's side door. She brings the seat forward and helps Ellis in behind it so he can rest on the bench seat. To her relief, the truck starts, and she hightails it out of there.

"Laura, I know you said not to try and stop you, but I have someone picked out," Ellis gasps.

"Not now," Laura tells him, picking up speed.

"You don't have to do this," he says, then yelps with a sudden sprang of fire in his skin.

Through the window, he watches the trees move by in a complete blur. The car comes to a stop and Ellis sits up. They are in the Western Pass park-and-ride by the woods. Laura helps him out of the car, ignoring his attempts to change her mind. He prods at her more when they breach the tree line. She avoids him, but he stops her a couple of steps down the path. "Please, are you certain about this?"

"It has to be me. Since that day at the cemetery, it was always supposed to be me."

The sincerity of her words silences him like it did the night before. He continues walking with her assistance. They step into the opening where JoJo lives. The two of them enter. Laura places him on the ground beside Bullet, who is wincing in pain; the hole in him bleeding.

Laura stares at the apple tree, ready to take a leap. Ellis grips Laura's hand in his, hard. Back to him, she confesses, "You were never wrong to bring me here, Ellis. Never wrong to find your way into my life or Frank's. He wouldn't have blamed you for wanting to give him what you thought you were giving me. You couldn't have known about his demons. And, maybe, he really is with Billy, and I have to believe that has made him happy. Whatever waits on the other side for me, can't be any worse than what I already know is waiting for me back out there."

Billy steps from the apple tree. He smears his palm in a swarm of color collecting on the floor from Laura's emotions and waves for someone else to join him. A dark outline of a man emerges from the apple tree. Billy fills the silhouette in until their vibrancy matches.

"Frank!" Laura bellows with relief.

Billy and Frank create a colorful pathway from the apple tree to Laura. Her face is a slobbered contortion of tears and joy. Frank plucks a purple apple from a branch and holds it out as an offering. Billy walks up the path and puts his hand out for his mother. Laura takes it and lets him guide her toward sacrifice.

Ellis crawls to the puddles left behind by her tears.

Laura stops at the apple tree and takes a deep breath. Frank places the apple in her hand. She closes her eyes and raises the neon fruit to her lips. Her mouth widens, teeth exposed and ready to bite into the unknown. Like that night in the road, she dangles before oblivion.

"No!" Ellis breaks Laura's concentration. She drops the apple. Ellis forces himself up, feverishly painting something with his back to Laura. His body stops creating and when he steps out of the way, he reveals an easel with a kaleidoscope canvas. He walks to her with shades of her own grief staining his hands and professes, "If what is beyond this place can bring a monster as easily as it can your son, or husband, there is no guarantee it is good in nature. Keep them alive here. Live with them here. Regrow your heart, Laura. Use forever to forgive yourself."

He places the color in her palms as she shakes her head. "No, you can't."

Ellis hugs her. The words fall from his mouth with soft tragedy.

"I'm tired of surviving, Laura. I just want to go home. But only if you are okay with being here."

Laura contemplates the weight of the moment. "If it sets you free, Ellis. Then, yes, I accept what comes with staying here. I'll be with them. That's what I want." She squeezes Ellis tighter. "You are loved, Ellis. I will miss you," Laura says, tenderly.

He lets go of her and caresses her pale cheek, leaving a smudge of blue on her face. He picks up the sickly Bullet and walks to the exit with Laura's multi-colored handprints on his shirt. Red tears turn chalk white on his cheeks as he steps through the opening, back into Hollow Hills. The sickness sets back in. He powers ahead into the woods with his fated companion cradled in his arms.

Laura stares out the window, catching Ellis's back as he vanishes into the world she no longer has any use for. Billy takes her hand. She gets to her knees and clutches him close. He wipes the tears off her face and walks her to the easel. She takes her finger and runs it along the canvas, rippling the colors already on it with the ones at her fingertips. Billy watches and imitates her motions. She turns to the apple tree and spots Frank smiling from where Bullet would usually sit. His heart, now visible and beating like the deer's. She looks down to Billy as he paints, his brow crunched in concentration. His heart morphs just the same.

The Beginning of Heartache

❦

Winter 1940

A gruff, but well-kept Michael Foster hurries to the front door. "Father Willan," he says, addressing a stout, balding man bundled up from the heavy snowfall. The priest's wire glasses dangle at the edge of his nose.

Michael shuts the door fast behind the priest to keep the cold out and welcomes him into the home. The walls are painted in fresh eggshell. Potted plants adorn various windowsills. Small signs of Christmas spirit are distributed amongst the scant decor. A modest Christmas tree stands beside a fireplace filled with crackling logs.

A woman's screams fight through the floor above the two men. Father Willan's concerned gaze meets the ceiling. He removes his gloves. Michael shakes his hand.

"Thank you, Father, for coming on such short notice," Michael resounds with gratitude, despite the fear coating his face.

Father Willan removes his hat and coat, handing them to Michael. "No storm shall halt the Lord's work, my son. Take me to her."

Michael sets the priest's belongings down on the couch and leads him through the kitchen, up a narrow staircase to a small hallway bordered by three closed doors. The agonized wails of the woman intensify as the two men proceed to the farthest door, passing several photos along the wall, one being a young Michael in a suit with a beautiful bride.

Michael opens the door, nearly knocking it into a fully frocked nun. She moves out of the way and on a bed against the wall is the woman from the wedding photo in the middle of childbirth. Her belly protrudes like a small Earth from the blanket on top of her. She writhes, blood on the sheets between her legs. Another nun is by her side, wiping her forehead with a wet rag. At the foot of the bed is an older doctor and his birthing assistant. The assistant rubs the woman's legs as the doctor examines the birth canal. "Mrs. Foster, I need you to push," the doctor instructs.

She grits her teeth and pushes with all her might. The pain electrifies her. She screams louder. Michael corrals Father Willan around the other side of the bed with him. The woman looks up at them, her face recoiled in struggle and pleads, "Please, Father, pray for my baby." Her voice breaks into a cry. The woman grips Michael's hand hard and lets out a visceral shriek that startles the room.

Father Willan opens his bible. "Dear Heavenly Father, I ask that you watch over your loving daughter, Joanne Foster, and son, Michael Foster, in their time of need, and through your almighty power grant them the serenity of a healthy, happy baby. Father, we call on you now..."

With every contraction comes a pain that dominates over the woman's entire body. She tries to keep her breath steady, as her stomach tightens with every new wave of distress.

Michael spots the worry on the birthing assistant's face. "Doctor, is everything okay? Is the baby okay?"

Joanne cries out again, more forceful than before. The doctor pulls his head back in front of the bed and barks orders to the room. "Sisters! We must reposition and keep her temperature down!" The doctor wipes the fog from his glasses. "My briefcase!"

The assistant grabs the doctor's medical case from the top of the dresser and runs it back to him. He opens it on the ground and pilfers through it for a vial and syringe. He inserts the syringe into the vial and draws back the depressor, filling the needle with solution. "We need space. Sister Grace, please show Mr. Foster and Father Willan out," the doctor orders with his eyes kept on Joanne.

Michael ignores him. Father Willan continues reciting his prayers. The doctor stands, syringe in hand to face Michael.

"I'm not going to leave my wife's side," Michael tells the doctor. He clutches her palm tighter.

The birthing assistance rationalizes with Michael. "Sir, please. We have little time to waste and can work more efficiently with less commotion."

Michael backs down. He eyes Father Willan to stop. The priest does, closing his bible and stepping away from the bed. Michael kneels once more. Joanne muscles through the pain, words barely escape her.

"Don't go, love."

"I will be right outside in the hallway, JoJo, waiting for you. Everything will be okay," Michael promises. He kisses her hand and then her head. "I love you," he says.

"Mr. Foster!" the doctor shouts.

Michael gets to his feet. Sister Grace leads Michael and Father Willan into the hallway where she has set up two wooden chairs for them. Father Willan takes a seat. Michael paces up and down the hallway, while his wife cries out from the other side of the wall.

"You mustn't fret, my son. God fills these walls. Let us pray,"

Father Willan says, holding out his hand to a frightened Michael.

Michael reaches for his hand and lowers to his knees before the cleric. Behind him lies the wedding picture on the wall and, beyond that, his wife's cries. Father Willan motions the sign of the cross with his free hand. Michael closes his eyes and bows his head.

"Dear Heavenly Father, I ask that your light and your love bestow itself upon this God-fearing home. I ask that your grace be given to young Michael and Joanne, devout children to your kingdom." The priest's conviction battles the moans from the room. Michael tightens his grip. "They bare your test, almighty father. They know your presence, as do I. Together, young Michael and I ask that your glorious hand penetrate the darkness of this midnight hour and carry into this world a bounty in the form of their child. Keep safe this man's legacy. Keep safe this man's wife. In the name of the father, the son, and the holy spirit, hear our prayer. Amen."

Joanne's cries go quiet.

"Amen," Michael says, lifting his head. His eyes open at the sound of a baby's cries.

He bolts to his feet and rushes through the bedroom door. Sister Grace holds the bloody baby in a towel, forlorn on her face.

"Is the baby alright?" Michael asks.

"Yes, a healthy baby boy," she replies.

The doctor stands in front of the bed, wiping the sweat from his brow. His birthing assistant sponges blood on the floor into a metal bin. Joanne lies motionless behind them. Her lifeless eyes open and unblinking in Michael's direction. Michael looks from her to the doctor, the truth settling into his soul. The doctor clears his throat. "I am sorry, Mr. Foster. We tried but..."

Michael buckles to his knees and breaks down. The sound of his grief rattles through the very foundation of the house and hearts of those inside it. His cries are echoed by the lungs of his newborn baby boy.

Home

Winter 2031

*E*llis makes it to his father's grave. He places Bullet down beside the tombstone, stroking the fur on his head, trying to comfort his friend the best he can. The pain rises and, with all his might, Ellis fights to breathe through it. The hair on his head begins to gray and then whitens. His spine weakens and lowers. Wrinkles grow across his face and hands. The strength leaves him. He collapses, his body finally catching up on all the time it has missed.

Bullet agonizes next to Ellis, but the deer doesn't whither like he does. Bullet's legs lengthen. His head widens. The antlers push from his skull to form an ornate structure of points and his fur goes white like an untouched patch of snow. Bullet gets to his feet, a fully grown stag, and stands over Ellis.

In the cold silence of the early afternoon, they gaze into each other's eyes. The fear seems to recede from Ellis's stare as his body travels beyond the length of his life. He manages a smirk. His head goes bald. The wrinkles worsen and his skin begins to crystalize and harden from rigor mortis. Parts of him sink from the weakening of his bones. His lungs expel a death rattle as his eyes widen toward the blue sky above him. Then, his head turns to face his father's grave. Deep and alive, his eyes work in tandem with what's left of his spirit. "Pa", he struggles to pronounce, a few sporadic tears roll down his face to the dirt. Moments later, his eyes still.

The White Stag brushes his nose against Ellis's face, licking his cheek. He nudges his body a few more times to no avail. The stag eventually decides to leave. Two rows away, it notices someone and lets up. A woman - standing at Billy and Frank's graves, putting a bouquet of flowers over them. It's Rose Whitley.

She focuses intently on the graves, noticing a black film building up around the edges of where Frank's tombstone touches the ground. The White Stag steps closer. Over her shoulder, she spots the deer. Slowly, she turns to face it. The White Stag calmly walks towards her. Initially startled, she soon becomes enamored by the strange beauty of the creature. Her hand held out, he approaches with caution and places his snout in her palm to lick her wrist. He looks up and the two of them share a quiet moment, before the animal walks off. Her eyes follow him. A few feet away, he stops and turns back to face her.

The White Stag walks from the cemetery to the edge of town, with Rose tailing behind. They stop by the small field nearest the playground. Most of the snow has melted away and the animal decides to graze in the grass while Rose waits on the sidewalk.

A man walks towards them in the distance. He wears an oversized jacket and trousers too long for his legs. Shoes covered in mud; he lopes along in the midday light alone. It's Moo. Rose comes into focus as he gets closer. He is stunned, almost stopping in his tracks at the sight of her.

"Rose," he utters.

286

Rose is floored. "Dad?"

Shocked, she turns back to the field. The White Stag is gone. Her bewilderment drifts back to Moo. Mere feet apart now, neither know what to say. The quiet between them thickens beyond discomfort. Moo cracks a grin. Rose follows suit. The tension in their bodies settles. Every agony, every regret, every moment of loneliness in their lives, slips away into the peace of a familiar face. And, momentarily, the two of them share a reprieve from the overwhelming weight of the universe.

Epilogue

Spring 1938

Daffodils, tulips, roses, azaleas, and violets decorate the bushes and grounds between the walking paths and neatly trimmed open grass of Kentwood Park. The sky is a perfect blue, blotted with the occasional cotton cloud. Dogs bark at pigeons cooing from between tree branches while squirrels look for some food to steal. Townsfolk come and go, holding picnics, enjoying lawn games, reading books. Children's laughter and delighted screams echo as they play tag. Hollow Hills is in full bloom for spring.

Under the shade of a huge tree that hugs the northern edge of the park sits a couple on a picnic blanket with a basket full of food. The woman is dressed in a beige sundress with a ribboned, wide-brimmed hat on her head. The man lay in front of her wearing form fitting slacks and a flannel shirt. His face is clean. His hair is slicked back. They enjoy a lunch of fresh fruit, cheese, and bread.

"I need to watch your mother make this one day, Mike," the woman says as she gulps down a lemonade.

"She doesn't like to give her secrets away, JoJo," Michael says.

"I'm her favorite, though," Joanne says, throwing a mischievous smile at him.

"Is that so?"

"It is, Michael Foster. You should have accepted that by now."

"If I wasn't so comfy right now, I'd..."

"You'd what?"

Michael smirks.

"That's more like it," Joanne says.

On a leisurely stroll down the path before the tree, walk a couple about the same age as them. Michael recognizes the man. "Arthur! Arthur Wayne, is that you?"

The man stops and squints at Michael. A distant memory finds its way to him and then, a giant smile fills his face. "Mike!"

Michael gets up and greets Arthur halfway. The two men shake hands.

"This is Gina, my wife," Arthur says, pointing at the lovely lady next to him. She's dressed to the nines in a gorgeous, flowered dress. Expensive sunglasses rest across the brim of her nose. Michael and Gina exchange pleasantries. Joanne joins them.

"And this is, JoJo, I mean, Joanne. The better half."

Joanne smiles. "A pleasure to meet you Arthur, Gina."

"Arthur and I went to grade school together, before his big brain got him accepted into a gifted children's school."

"Impressive," Joanne says.

"Mike, here, is being silly. My brain isn't big. It's gigantic."

"Not as gigantic as his ego," Gina interjects.

Loud laughter erupts in the group.

"So, tell me, how has life treated you?" Michael asks.

"Quite well, actually. That school led to some wonderful things.

One being, Gina. We met in an accelerated physics program. Now, we are both working on a team at Herne. The plant across the way in Swift Landing."

"That's great, Arthur. I'm happy for you."

"Yourself?" Arthur inquires.

"Good. Joanne and I met at mass after her family moved to town. I'm working the docks, which keeps me busy. Pay isn't so bad. Hopefully make foreman one day. We've got ourselves a pretty simple life, but we love it."

Gina gives Arthur a hurried stare.

"Mike, I don't mean to cut this short, but we were just walking through to meet my parents for lunch."

"No, no. Please, wouldn't want to keep you from family on such a lovely day," Michael says.

"The four of us, we should get together for dinner. What are you two up to next Friday night? We could meet at the Roundabout, 6:30?"

Michael and Joanne share an agreeable look with one another.

"Sounds perfect," Joanne says.

"Wonderful," Arthur cheers.

They all say their farewells and Arthur and Gina continue down the path to the park exit.

"We should probably get going ourselves," Joanne suggests.

Michael looks up at the sky. "Sun is sitting a little low," he says.

The two of them gather their belongings into the basket. They take the same path as Arthur and Gina to exit the park. Out onto the sidewalk, Michael turns toward the direction home, but Joanne stands still, staring at the cliffs in the distance. Michael stops and turns back.

"What is it, love? Everything okay?" His eyes search for an answer on her face.

"I don't want to go home and do chores. It's too beautiful out."

Michael joins her where she stands. He tries to follow her gaze. "What would you rather do?"

She points to the cliff. "Go up there and watch the water kiss the sky."

Michael glares at her intently, a deep desire evident in her eyes. Then, he grabs her hand. "What my JoJo wants, my JoJo gets." He kisses her on the cheek. She grows pink.

They cross the street and set off in the direction of Western Pass. By the time they arrive at the cliff, a quarter of the sun has slipped behind the horizon. The colors in the sky are vast and vivid. Deep fuchsia and thick cream determinately wash the blue away. Michael sets the blanket down close to the edge. Joanne takes a seat while Michael stands, hands on his waist, taking in the breadth of the sunset.

"Come. Sit. I'm cold," Joanne says.

Michael lowers behind her and pulls her between his legs. Joanne takes his arms around her body to feel his warmth. He nestles his face upon her shoulder. They sit and watch the radiant fires in the sky become slowly swallowed by night.

To Be Continued...

*T*his is for those stuck in the hole, where grief grows in the shadows of our bones and latches onto the heart like a cancer. It's for those in that empty, seemingly endless space between loss and healing. That place where all thoughts fall victim to the aches adhered to the dirt our shoes pull from the graves we visit. Each of us on that path alone, toward a day where the sun seems a bit warmer than the one before. It'll come. At different moments for us all. It really does take that precious resource we never have enough of with those we love but seem to have an abundance of after we lose them – Time. With time, it gets better. Not perfect. Not always fully complete or repaired, but better. And until it does, feel free to look into the below if you need help.

Grief, Loss, Counseling, and Prevention Resources

https://www.samhsa.gov/
https://www.griefresourcenetwork.com/crisis-center/hotlines/
https://www.aa.org/
https://adultchildren.org/
https://www.counseling.org/
http://thesanctuaryforgrief.org/

National Suicide Prevention Lifeline – 1.800.273.8255

Timeless Gardens & Other Beautiful Miseries Playlist

Leaving on a Jet Plane – Peter, Paul and Mary
Eleanor Rigby – The Beatles
Never Going Back Again – Fleetwood Mac
The Hucklebuck – Chubby Checker
Dream A Little Dream of Me – The Mamas & The Papas
'Round Midnight – Miles Davis
500 Miles – Peter, Paul and Mary
Everybody's Gotta Live – Love
Blue Monday – Fats Domino
The Christmas Song – Nat King Cole
Behind the Lines – Genesis
She's Not There – The Zombies
Lemon Tree – Peter, Paul and Mary
So What – Miles Davis
California Dreamin' – The Mamas & The Papas
Get Back – The Beatles
For the Love of Money – The O'Jays
I Dig Rock and Roll Music – Peter, Paul and Mary
Intermission Riff – Stan Kenton
The Thrill is Gone – B.B. King
Last Dance – George Clinton
Guerilla Radio – Rage Against the Machine
The Letter – The Box Tops
Sanctuary – Miles Davis
Heresy – Nine Inch Nails
If I Had Wings – Peter, Paul and Mary
Stormy Weather – Etta James
All Things Must Pass – George Harrison
Leaving on a Jet Plane – Peter, Paul and Mary

listen on Spotify

Ellis's Book List

Stuart Little by E.B. White
The Time Machine by H.G. Wells
The Spy Who Came in from the Cold by John le Carré
The Little Island by Margaret Wise Brown
Cujo by Stephen King
The Clocks by Agatha Christie
The Count of Monte Cristo by Alexandre Dumas
Holes by Louis Sachar

CPSIA information can be obtained
at www.ICGtesting.com
Printed in the USA
LVHW082326220422
716980LV00016B/717/J